D1236079

EAT
THE
RICH

ANDREW RIVAS

Copyright © 2020 Andrew Rivas
All rights reserved.
www.andrew-rivas.com

This is a work of fiction. Names, characters, businesses, places, events, locales, and incidents are either the products of the author's imagination or used in a fictitious manner. Any resemblance to actual persons, living or dead, or actual events is entirely coincidental.

Note: **Eating** **the rich** *is a metaphor. For legal purposes, the author of this work is not suggesting that you literally* **eat the rich**.

EAT
THE
RICH

*Quand les pauvres n'auront plus rien à
manger, ils mangeront les riches!*

—Jean-Jacques Rousseau

When the people shall have nothing more to eat, they will eat the rich.

—Translation

Episode 1

Tacos de Lengua

THE TONGUE IN front of me is from the noted racist, bigot, and hypocrite, David White. At the time of his death, his estimated net worth was one hundred and twelve million dollars.

Today, we will be making tacos de lengua, or at least my version of tacos de lengua, which is traditionally made with beef tongue. I was given the following recipe by one of my friends whose abuela has been cooking lengua for years. Because beef tongues usually weigh a couple of pounds and David's weighs only a tenth of one, I've had to make some adjustments to the recipe. Since I'm not a professional or even an amateur chef, you might have to make your own adjustments when you cook your own.

You'll need the following ingredients to prepare David White's tongue:

- 3-4 cloves of garlic
- ¼ onion
- 1-2 bay leaves
- 1 carrot, peeled and chopped

Before you start, do some research on televangelist David White. Note how his grandfather, Jackson White, was a slave owner whose tobacco plantation closed after the Civil War. Read up on how Leland

White, his father, was a pastor whose reported net worth was one and a half million dollars in 1962, the year in which David was born. Listen to the words that Leland spoke, words he repeated to anyone who would listen, words recorded for posterity, where he advocated for segregation and isolationism and "America First". Take in the history of David White's family, his legacy, that enabled him to take his father's inheritance and build an empire.

The first step is to fill a large pot two-thirds full with water. Crush the garlic cloves the way the rich crush the poor and less fortunate and disenfranchised under their heel. They do so metaphorically; crush the garlic cloves literally. Dice the onion. Put the crushed garlic, the bay leaves, the diced onion, and the chopped carrot into the pot. Put David's tongue in last. Bring the water to a boil and then reduce to a simmer. Cover and cook the tongue for an hour or until tender. It may take longer than expected. David used his tongue, his voice, often to ill effect. He used it to spread hate. He used it to profit off of that hate. Boil the tongue until the hate dissolves away.

Remove the tongue from the pot and let it cool. Using your fingers, remove the tough, lightly colored exterior of the tongue. You could use a knife, but you want to feel the meat slip between your fingers. While you're doing this, play a video of David preaching the "seed faith" doctrine: the belief that donations to his church were a form of "seed" that would grow and be rewarded back to those who donated. That by giving him money, his followers were practicing their faith; that by believing in God and believing in David, his followers would be rewarded financially and physically in this world and beyond measure in the next; that by amassing millions and millions of dollars, he was doing the Lord's work and somehow benefiting humanity. Read up on prosperity theology, or the belief that the rich are rich because they have been blessed by God, and not because they fleece and bleed the poor.

Throw the tough exterior away. The same way you threw David's body away. All reduced to trash, to ash. Save the tender meat from the inside of the tongue. Think back to 2006, after Hurricane Katrina, when David refused to open his megachurch to the thousands of people displaced because of flooding. Remember how he called them "filth" and "nonbelievers" from his yacht. Google some photos of the destruction caused by the hurricane and then look at the pictures of David's empty mega-church surrounded by people at their lowest point, countless people whom David could have helped. Easily. Not only did he not help them, he chose not to in order to spite them. Note how little meat there actually is. Maybe enough to make one taco. Note how something so small could make such a big difference. Note how David chose to use his influence to hurt people. So many people. Over and over again.

Slice the tongue into thin strips, longways. To fry the tongue, you'll need vegetable oil and a frying pan. Sauté the slices until they are a light brown. Remove the strips from the pan. Cube the strips of tongue by cutting them lengthwise and crosswise. Season with salt and pepper. Listen to David call immigrants "invaders." Listen to him gripe about how he has to hear other people speak languages that aren't English. Listen to him say that certain kids belong in cages, and that they deserve it because their parents broke the law. Listen to him explain that we have to "take care of real Americans first." Now that the meat is prepared, gather the ingredients for the taco itself:

- Corn tortilla
- Pinch of diced cilantro
- Feta
- Diced red onion
- Store-bought salsa verde (relish in the fact that David would be furious that any part of the taco was store-bought)

You can figure this part out, can't you? Put the dang meat in the tortilla. Listen to the speech where David preached that homosexuals were corrupting the sanctity of marriage. Listen to how he called them deranged, depraved; listen to how he claimed erroneously that they were kidnapping children and converting them to homosexuality. Note how he gave this speech in November of 2017, weeks before a string of serial assaults against homosexuals began in Louisiana, one of which resulted in a death. Forget the name of the man who murdered Frank Wallace, but remember that David called the murderer "a good man" and said he shouldn't be imprisoned for "an honest mistake."

Dress the taco. Listen to the speech David gave on January 27th, 2018 where he rallied his flock against a mosque that had opened up twenty miles from his megachurch in Lafayette. Listen, really listen, to how he claimed that "ISIS is setting up shop in the real America." Remember that he called Islam a disease and that he compared Muslims to rats and said "that if someone doesn't do something, the same thing that happened to New York on 9/11 could happen here."

Someone did do something. A man threw two Molotov cocktails in through the front door of the mosque on January 30th, 2018. Forget the name of the man who threw the bottles, but remember the names of the three human beings that were murdered by the man. That burned to death while in a place of worship. A place of peace. Omar Khan. Rahim Parekh and his daughter, Emily.

Eat the damn thing. It tastes better than you would expect, knowing where it came from. That part doesn't matter so much—the eating itself. The more important part is that it is eaten. Chew the meat that used to be David White and turn it into paste. Swallow it and digest it with your bile. Then crap him out. Ashes to ashes. Dust to dust. Human crap to literal crap. That's what he deserves, what he was always meant to be. David White's millions can't help him now.

Remember that, at the start of the NOVA-90 outbreak in 2019, David White refused to cancel any of his weekly *Rising Sun* shows. While every other nonessential business was closing, David White argued that his church was an essential business, and kept packing his megachurch full every Sunday. He closed his church to the Hurricane Katrina survivors, but he remained open during a pandemic. Remember the Easter mass that was televised live, where he told his congregation that God was speaking through him, that the breath of God purified any souls that walked through the doors to his church, and that God himself had told him to keep his church open and that He would keep White's congregation safe.

It's impossible to tell how many people were indirectly infected by

David White, but we do know now that in the month he fought to keep his church open, three hundred and twenty of his flock were infected with NOVA-90 and eighteen died. It's impossible to know how many people *those* people infected, how many they went out and killed because of White downplaying the virus, but we can pin those deaths on him. Those deaths were preventable but White wanted his tithe.

This isn't a metaphor. Not anymore.

If you liked this recipe, consider donating to RAICES. Link in the description.

Until next time. Stay hungry.

[reddit.com]

▲ **4** ▼

r/videos • Posted by u/ashwhateverr ⊗ 1 year ago

EAT THE RICH EPISODE 1 - Tacos de lengua
youtube.com/watch? . . .⤶

SORT BY **NEW** ▼

marksarcophagus ⊗ 5 points • 1 year ago
Is this real?
⊟ **Reply Share Report Save**

> **throwaway34324243** ⊗ 7 points • 1 year ago
> fake.
> ⊟ **Reply Share Report Save**

> **sovereigncitizen1040** ⊗ 3 points • 1 year ago
> fake, i think
> ⊟ **Reply Share Report Save**

neato_burrit0_wsc ⊗ 2 points • 1 year ago
Alright idea, poor execution. Tongue looks nothing like a human
tongue. Feta on a taco? Gross.
⊟ **Reply Share Report Save**

> **xxnarutosmokesbluntsxx420** ⊗ 4 points • 1 year ago
> feta is delicious you uncultured SWINE
> ⊟ **Reply Share Report Save**

PM_ME_PICS_OF_UR_FEET ⊠ -2 points • 1 year ago
show ur feet
⊡ **Reply Share Report Save**

truamer1c4nsince1972 ⊠ 0 points • 1 year ago
Disgusting. Advocating murder against a man of God? Reported.
⊡ **Reply Share Report Save**

redpillz4everyone69 ⊠ -6 points • 1 year ago
no one cares about ur politics u dumb bitch
⊡ **Reply Share Report Save**

8 |

[twitter.com]

Chrissie Norman @mothers_4_jesus1978 · Feb 13

So excited to be at the #DawnoftheRisingSun show
at the Arboretum Theater in New Orleans! Can't wait
to see @therealdavidwhite in person for the first time!

10:13 AM · Feb 13, 2022 · **Twitter for iPhone**

---

2 Replies   3 Retweets   7 Likes

Chrissie Norman @mothers_4_jesus1978 · Feb 13
Replying to **@mothers_4_jesus1978**

Unbelievable performance by the @blessedtones! I
could literally feel the word of God move through me!
Already worth the price of admission!

10:52 AM · Feb 13, 2022 · **Twitter for iPhone**

---

1 Reply   2 Retweets   11 Likes

Chrissie Norman @mothers_4_jesus1978 · Feb 13
Replying to **@mothers_4_jesus1978**

Where is @therealdavidwhite? He was supposed to
go on at 11. Staff are making excuses for him
not starting. Is he okay? Praying for him!

11:24 AM · Feb 13, 2022 · **Twitter for iPhone**

---

4 Replies   5 Retweets   3 Likes

Chrissie Norman @mothers_4_jesus1978 · Feb 13
Replying to **@mothers_4_jesus1978**

@therealdavidwhite is this how you treat your loyal
followers? You couldn't even come on stage
to apologize for cancelling?!?!? Even if you're sick,
a lot of people came a long way to see you . . .

1:03 PM · Feb 13, 2022 · **Twitter for iPhone**

---

9 Replies   3 Retweets   11 Likes

Chrissie Norman @mothers_4_jesus1978 · Feb 13
Replying to **@mothers_4_jesus1978**

@therealdavidwhite I paid $44 for to see you and
even more on gas to drive to freakin' New Orleans . . .
I WANT MY MONEY BACK!!!!

4:19 PM · Feb 13, 2022 · **Twitter for iPhone**

---

10 Replies   15 Retweets   22 Likes

[facebook.com]

Posts

PRAYERS FOR DAVID WHITE
April 3 at 2:23 PM

To all you White fans out there!!!!!
PLEASE keep David in your prayers and consider donating
to #thechurchofwhite to speed up David's recovery!!!!!
(link in about section of this group)
Show David the power of our faith!!!!!!!

778 likes   224 Comments   204 Shares

Like   **Comment**   **Share**

PRAYERS FOR DAVID WHITE
March 20 at 2:23 PM

To all you White fans out there!!!!!
Sally White during the Sunday #RisingSunTogether show
thanked #thechurchofwhite for their donations and for
keeping David in their prayers!!!!! David is healing
quickly, she said, but needs more time!!!! For the
foreseeable future she will be giving his sermon
and spreading the word of God to
#thechurchofwhite!!! More updates soon!!!!!!

669 Likes   186 Comments   193 Shares

Like   **Comment**   **Share**

PRAYERS FOR DAVID WHITE
February 27 at 2:23 PM

To all you White fans out there!!!!!
Sally White during the Sunday #RisingSunTogether show
explained why David missed the #Dawnoftherisingsun show
and the sermons since! He is sick, she said, but strong and
should return soon!!!!Let's come together and PRAY and
PROVE that the power and love of God can heal the
truly righteous!!!! Consider donating to #thechurchofwhite
(link in the about section of this group) to prove our faith
in David and in the Lord our GOD!!!!!

955 Likes   350 Comments   599 Shares

Like   **Comment**   **Share**

[reddit.com]

▲ **72** ▼

r/thechurchofwhite • Posted by u/gospelofwhite1975 ⊗ 1 year ago

Is Pastor White okay?

Sally White has been doing the weekly Rising Sun Together shows for the past six weeks. He's cancelled three shows since February, with no satisfactory answer why. He hasn't been seen in public since February 9th. No one's said anything about it other than he's sick. But if so, why hasn't his twitter been updated since early Feb? Why hasn't he posted a video on the church's instagram showing everyone he's okay? He's in my prayers, obviously, but I'm really worried about him. Has anyone seen anything I somehow missed?

SORT BY **BEST** ▼

god1sanamerican_000 ⊗ 55 points • 1 year ago
Have faith. If something was wrong Sally would've said something.
⊡ **Reply Share Report Save**

> **faithbasedcontent** ⊗ 33 points • 1 year ago
> True. White's teaching is all about faith. Have faith, keep David in your prayers, and everything will work out.
> ⊡ **Reply Share Report Save**

christianm0ms4white ⊗ 48 points • 1 year ago
I hope Sally isn't taking advantage of his flock. What if something

happened to him and Sally hasn't said anything? I don't really know anything about her.
⊡ **Reply Share Report Save**

> **grandpa_of4_** ⊗ 4 points · 1 year ago
> sally white AKA sally eidelman is a fukn jew what do you expect read up on her father's ties to the media wake up to the fact that this is a g-ddmn TAKEOVER
> ⊡ **Reply Share Report Save**

donations4white ⊗ 15 points · 1 year ago
Donate to the Church of White **here**! Keep David in your prayers by seeding your faith! All will work out in the end!!!
⊡ **Reply Share Report Save**

wakeupsheepl3 ⊗ 2 points · 1 year ago
have they finalyl got to him? the deep state? He's been in there crosshairs 4 yrs . . ..
⊡ **Reply Share Report Save**

[instagram.com]

⊠

thechurchofwhite ✓ • Follow . . .

thechurchofwhite Picture of David recovering by
the pool! Thanks for all the well wishes! Keep
David in your prayers!

1y

kpopstanley Isn't this an old photo?

1y   11 likes   Reply
——   Hide Replies

      annabannnnnnnana99 @kpopstanley yup. from
      Jan 2019. they didn't even delete it.

      1y   7 likes   Reply

saracesaragarcia Thank GOD!! Love you David!!

1y   3 likes   Reply

1shot1killnoremorse DAVIDS A REAL AMERICAN
UNLIKE THOSE DAMN DO NOTHING
DEMCRATS!!!

1y   Reply

cheezybr33zy donating to #thechurchofwhite so God

knows David is loved!!! plant those seeds and
fortune grows!!!

1y   Reply

aswerycruelproduction open your eyes . . .
#whereisdavidwhite?

1y   Reply

18,040 views
1y

[reddit.com]

▲ **450** ▼

r/conspiracy · Posted by u/flatearthbelieber ⊗ 1 year ago

David White: Is this a Shelly Miscavige situation?

With the roles reversed. Hasn't been seen in public for more than two months. His wife Sally has taken over all his shows and has pushed the narrative "that he's sick" the entire time. Hasn't updated his twitter, posted a video, nothing. Higher-ups in "the church" are being told to tell the media that they've seen him, but privately they admit they haven't. If he's sick, why not post a short video to squash the rumors? If he's dead, why not just admit it as such? Somethings fucky . . .

SORT BY **BEST** ▼

jacksbileduct ⊗ 212 points · 1 year ago
TBF, Shelly Miscavige has been missing since 2007, David has only been missing for two months. More than likely he is sick but they're trying to downplay how sick he actually is.
⊡ **Reply Share Report Save**

> **gorilla_radio88** ⊗ 128 points · 1 year ago
> you know you're in R/conspiracy, right bud? cut it out with the rationale answers . . .
> ⊡ **Reply Share Report Save**

>> **vaypemancave** ⊗ 94 points · 1 year ago
>> found the mobile user

⊡ **Reply Share Report Save**

legallizeeveryth1ng ⊗ 127 points · 1 year ago
seems plausible but this is the church we're talking
about, keep your eyes open don't rule anything
out
⊡ **Reply Share Report Save**

MKMichelobUltra ⊗ 166 points · 1 year ago
not saying there's not something fucky but no way church
of white is as shady as scientology . . . they're not telling the
truth about david but sally didn't murder david like david
murdered shelly
⊡ **Reply Share Report Save**

    dabstate2004 ⊗ 23 points · 1 year ago
    HISTORY REPEATS ITSELF . . . DAVID & SHELLY
    > SALLY & DAVID . . .. NOT A COINCIDENCE
    ALL CHURCHES ARE CULTS STARTING WITH
    JUDISM . . .
    ⊡ **Reply Share Report Save**

rainbowchemtrails___ ⊗ 78 points · 1 year ago
Anyone else see that Eat The Rich video on youtube? Think there's
any chance that's real?
⊡ **Reply Share Report Save**

(Show more comments)

[twitter.com]

Trending · #WhereIsDavidWhite · 3,192 tweets

Nadia Swindley @princesspaella · April 19

THE FOLLOWERS OF WHITE DESERVE AN
ANSWER. TELL US THE TRUTH, SALLY
#WhereIsDavidWhite

---

4 Replies   **14 Retweets**   **11 Likes**

John Washington @defnotarushnbot1776 · April 19

The DEEP STATE Illuminati REPTILIAN
GOVERNMENT took out a CHRISTIAN ICON . . .
THIS IS WAR #WhereIsDavidWhite

Reply   **Retweet**   **Like**

Karl Barx @w00fw00fcomrade · April 19

Anyone else find it weird that they call themselves
"The Church of White", "Followers of White," etc?
Saying the quiet part out loud . . . #WhereIsDavidWhite

---

1 Reply   **25 Retweets**   **19 Likes**

Grace S. @graceofgod558630 · April 19

Not everything is a conspiracy. Have faith that
David is okay. I don't need to know
#WhereisDavidWhite because I have faith.

2 Replies   1 Retweet   1 Like

Anna Salvatore @salva_anna_cali · April 19

Looking for a guy with a good dick for sex and
relationships! Call me on whatsap

#ChurchofWhite #DavidWhite #WhereisDavidWhite
#SallyWhite #RisingSun #FuckDavidWhite
#PrayersforDavidWhite

2 Replies   1 Retweet   1 Like

SKELLY TON @dal4irz0ne80085 · April 19

Who cares where tf that asshole is . . . fr
Maybe he's hiding in his fat ass mega church
while people starve on the street . . .
#WhereIsDavidWhite

Reply   2 Retweets   3 Likes

Episode 2

Andouille

HEY ZOOMERS AND boomers, Ash here with another episode of *Eat the Rich*. Today we will be making Andouille with "Dirty" Harry Cadejo, the CEO of Come Correct, the biggest manager of private prisons and detention centers in the United States. At the time of his death his net worth was seventy-four-point-two million dollars. Now, he wasn't as rich as David White, but it's not about the numbers here at Eat the Rich. It's about how they made their money. And Harry Cadejo, who definitely gave himself the nickname "Dirty Harry," made his money by turning his prisons into businesses.

"Now, Ash," you might say. "Wouldn't Andouille have made more sense for David White, seeing as how David lived in Louisiana and Andouille's a cajun dish?" And to that I say, who the heck cares? David was a silver-tongued weasel who hated immigrants, so I made his dang tongue into tacos. Harry is the one who turned his prisons into revolving-door meat processing plants. So he gets made into sausage. Do you get the metaphor, or do I need to spoon-feed it to you?

I won't apologize for being abrasive. Not all of us on the same side. Some people want to eat the rich, some people only want to feed them. If you're one of the former, you'll understand where I'm coming from. If you're one of the latter, then I don't give a hoot about your feelings.

Now, as I said in the first episode, I'm not a chef. I'm not a butcher. The recipe calls for one to two pounds of fatty pork shoulder, so I looked at a diagram of pork cuts and then cut off a slice of Harry where I thought it made sense. This isn't about a reproducible recipe, this isn't about making a tasty sausage. It's about holding the rich accountable and turning them into excrement. That's where I'm coming from. Harry was a mountain of a man, and I'm not one for body shaming, but there was plenty of Harry left over after I carved off a slice. I threw him in a meat freezer and maybe I'll do another recipe with him later.

Before you prepare Harry, it's important to know why I chose him for context. America is one of the only developed countries in the world that allows private entities to run prisons. Disregarding the myriad other problems with America's prison industrial complex, private prisons are a special kind of scum. The simplest explanation for why they eat ass (and not in a good way) is that they prioritize profit over rehabilitation. It's not about helping people reform and reintegrate; it's not about minimizing recidivism. It's about keeping the highest number of people imprisoned for as long as you can so you can make a dirty buck off them. That's the crux of it.

To turn Dirty Harry into Andouille, you'll need the following:
- Meat grinder
- Hog casings
- Butcher's string
- 2 pounds of Dirty Harry's shoulder
- 3 ½ pounds of actual pork
- 1 onion (diced)
- 2 tablespoon kosher salt
- ½ tablespoon cayenne pepper
- 4 tablespoons minced fresh garlic
- ½ tablespoon paprika
- ½ tablespoon dried thyme
- ½ cup chilled red wine

It's difficult to know where to start. Come Correct is a business, first and foremost. "Saving the government money" becomes synonymous with "cutting corners at the expense of prisoners and staff." According to research done by The Sentencing Project, Come Correct's employees earn an average of seven thousand dollars less than those employed by the government and receive sixty-two fewer hours of training (citation in the description of this video). This leads to less qualified guards, higher turnover, and overall decreased security. The Justice Department, in a 2018 report, found that Come Correct's prisons have a 37 percent higher rate of inmate-on-inmate assaults, twice as many inmate-on-staff assaults, and twice as many illicit weapons. The report also found that Come Correct's prisons regularly failed to ensure inmates were receiving medical care, which is monitored by the Bureau of Prisons. Twelve percent of Come Correct's prisons have not had a full-time doctor employed in the last three months.

Forgive me for getting into the weeds here with statistics. Some people are only convinced by hard facts, by numbers, but maybe I shouldn't pander to those people. They're never going to be convinced that Harry deserved to die; they're never going to be convinced of anything that opposes their already warped views. To them I'll just be fake news. Maybe I shouldn't be convincing anyone that Harry deserved to be made into sausage; maybe I should focus on reminding myself why I chose this particular pig.

I don't know what this series is yet. I'll still put citations in the description, because crediting people's work and providing evidence that supports my argument are both important. But maybe it shouldn't be part of the video. I'm figuring it out as I go along, as I'm sure you are as well. Maybe we'll find out together.

These are among the least damnable things I could find about Come Correct. I haven't even started to talk about the fact that private prisons in general arguably don't even save the government money; in some cases, they cost even more. Any money "saved" doesn't benefit the government; it doesn't benefit the public. It only benefits the private prisons themselves. There's a reason they're labelled as for-profit. I haven't even mentioned the lobbying efforts to change laws to target low-income minorities. I haven't even begun to talk about the detention centers.

Dice the pork and Dirty Harry into one-third-inch cubes. Take the two piles of meat and mix the two pigs together until they're indistinguishable from each other. It doesn't work; the meats look much different from one another. Use a mortar and pestle to grind the garlic, the onion, the salt, the spices, the thyme, all of that. Rub the mixture onto the meat cubes, really rub it in there, then cover and put it in the fridge for a day or two.

While you're doing this, listen to Eff the Police and Killing in the Name on repeat. It's *extremely* on the nose, but you shouldn't care. It's not subtle, but it'll make you feel good, I promise.

There's the Kids for Cash scandal, which doesn't have anything to do with Come Correct, but it shows how dirty the system can get. Two judges in Pennsylvania were found to be sentencing juveniles disproportionately to for-profit prisons to increase occupancy at said prisons in exchange for money. Literally selling children to the prison system. For-profit prisons all over America lobby Congress; ten million dollars since 1989 has gone towards lawmakers who toughen drug laws to make sure the prisons are fuller than ever before. A for-profit prison in Arizona in 2019 sued the state for having a lack of prisoners, feeling so entitled to jailing whomever they could that they legally attacked the state.

"But Ash," you say. "Private prisons are bad, sure. But why did Dirty Harry deserve to die? Specifically him?" I'm getting there, I promise.

Days later, time in which you've researched private prisons so you'd have material for this video, put the meat in the freezer for a couple of hours. Then grind the meat the way—wait, I've already made that metaphor. Getting sloppy. Put the meat through the meat grinder. Mix it up with your hands. Really feel Harry squish through your fingers. Mix it up until the two pigs are indistinguishable from one another. Then put the meat back in the freezer until it measures about 30 degrees Fahrenheit.

Harry famously said, in audio leaked from a fundraiser for a pedophile politician whose name I won't mention but you could easily google, that recidivism is Come Correct's bread and butter. That inmates imprisoned at Come Correct's facilities are 31 percent more likely to return to prison within two years of their release than prisoners from government-run facilities. That annually, Come Correct makes twenty-five thousand dollars profit, on average, from every prisoner in their prisons.

Soak the hog casings in water for five to ten minutes. Drain them. Rinse the casings with cold water, then drain them again. Check for holes in the casings; you don't want any Harry to leak out. You want him packed nice and tight. Pack the casings tight, manually. Use your hands. It's important to use your hands. Pack the meat as tight as you can. After fifteen to twenty inches, tie the ends off with butcher's string. Repeat until you run out of pig.

Dirty Harry did everything in his power to bleed his prisoners dry. He charged the prisoners fifty cents per day to borrow books from the prison library; he charged them eighty cents per minute to use the prison phones; he charged them fifty cents a minute for visitation; he lowered standards for prison food so low that rotting food and maggots became a common occurrence, which forced prisoners to eat exclusively from the commissary, then took a 25 percent commission when prisoners added money to their commissary funds. He overbooked cells then charged prisoners a fee to stay in rooms with the proper amount of prisoners; he contracted out prisoners to politicians to cold-call constituents, to fight local wildfires, to do construction and maintenance work on the prisons themselves, all the while paying the prisoners seventy cents an hour. This list is not inclusive, but you get the point.

Hang the links for an hour to let them dry. Sterilize a needle and pop any air pockets you see. You don't want the links to burst when you smoke them; no, that would be bad. You *could* cook them in an oven but Andouille is typically smoked. If you have a smoker, smoke the links for four hours or until they reach an internal temperature of 160 degrees Fahrenheit. Check the temperature with a meat thermometer. You don't want to get sick from Dirty Harry.

Finally, the most recent and egregious of Harry's sins. Detention centers. Under the previous administration, detention increased drastically, and Come Correct entered into a contract with the US government to make sure their prisons are where these people are kept. They received over two billion dollars in 2017 alone to run these detention centers (more recent figures have not been made public). In what is definitely a coincidence, Come Correct has spent over a hundred million dollars lobbying senators and congresspeople who make immigration laws.

Come Correct receives seven hundred dollars per day per "inmate." But where does that money go? It has come out that it hasn't gone towards basic necessities. The immigrants detained are not provided with toiletries (such as toothpaste or soap), running water (for showers and toilets), or clothes. They're being kept in literal cages instead of cells, herded together like animals, their numbers far exceeding what is generally considered safe for the space provided. Parents are not provided with formula for infants, children are not provided with education or anything resembling recreation, no one is provided with beds (only space blankets). Where is that money going, if not for Dirty Harry's pockets?

At any one time, tens of thousands of people are being held by ICE. Over the past few years, more than fifteen thousand children have been separated from their parents. More than sixty five people have died in custody (that we know of), among them children and literal infants. Earlier this year, when asked about the lack of oversight at his detention centers and the horrible conditions, Harry Cadejo laughed, saying that none of that mattered. That profits have never been better and if those people didn't want to be locked up, they shouldn't have broken the law.

As an aside, you may think I've forgotten about what's left of the bodies of David White and Harry Cadejo. I have not. They are both being stored for a future recipe. They will be eaten. They will be returned to the people. Nothing will go to waste. Rest assured, they will be eaten.

Before we consume of Dirty Harry's flesh, before we take our unholy capitalist communion, we should touch briefly on how Mr. Cadejo reacted to the NOVA-90 pandemic. While federal and state prisons made some amount of effort to curb NOVA-90 infections and deaths by commuting nonviolent offenders' sentences and releasing them from prisons to lessen population density, Harry made no such concessions. Prisons that were already overpopulated stayed that way, and PPE that was shipped to Harry's prisons for staff were secretly seized and disappeared. Cadejo's staff said that for the duration of the pandemic, they never saw a single mask or test. We can assume that those masks and tests were sold on the black market somewhere, but I'm wary of making claims that I can't adequately prove, so take that with a grain of salt.

There are no official numbers for how many of CC's prisoners and staff were infected with or died of NOVA-90 during the pandemic, but analyses from several different institutions released after the fact seem to agree on somewhere around a hundred thousand infections and two to three thousand deaths, which per-prison is triple the national average. Even more concerning might be CC's detention centers, which reported literally no infections and no deaths during the pandemic, which is a statistical impossibility.

Keep in mind that the following information is unsubstantiated, but it's far from the normal conspiracy theories you see on the internet. It comes from several individuals across multiple websites, Twitch and YouTube streamers, anonymous posters on 4chan, even users of a Facebook group for drone enthusiasts who flew their drones over a detention facility in New Mexico and captured footage of mass graves being dug and filled on land owned by Come Correct. This was August of 2019, five months after the first case of NOVA-90 in the States. One grave was already filled with over a hundred bodies and several more were being dug. Mainstream news ran the story for less than a day before they unceremoniously dropped it. The pictures were scrubbed from the sites they were posted to and the people that posted them were fined and slapped with gag orders.

Sounds far-fetched, I know. That's not how the internet works, you tell me. But all you know is that that's not how the internet works *for you.*

Andouille is typically added to dishes like gumbo and jambalaya, but I simply ran out of time. Other things came up, preparations for future recipes, that sort of thing. So I just slapped the dang thing on a bun with some green peppers, onions, and Creole mustard. It tastes . . . off. Well, no, that's not it. It tastes good. The spices and toppings, especially the mustard, hide a lot of the taste. But the texture is off. Something is not necessarily right with it. But what can you expect with such dirty meat? Even with all the preparation, you know where it came from. It's tainted.

I'll say it again. That part doesn't matter so much—the eating itself. The more important part is that it is eaten. Chew the meat that used to be Harry Cadejo and turn it into paste. Swallow it and digest it with your bile. Then crap him out. Ashes to ashes. Dust to dust. Human crap to literal crap. That's what he deserves, what he was always meant to be. Harry Cadejo's millions can't help him now.

This isn't a metaphor. Not any more. With enough people, with enough repetition, we can turn it into a mantra. Into a rallying cry. Eat the rich. They don't deserve what they've hoarded. None of them are safe.

If you liked this recipe, consider donating to any of the charities recommended by the Center for Prison Reform. Link in the description.

Until next time. Stay hungry.

[reddit.com]

▲ 71 ▼
r/videos · Posted by u/ashwhateverr ⊠ 11 months ago

EAT THE RICH EPISODE 2 - Andouille
youtube.com/watch? . . .↗

SORT BY **NEW** ▼

staygoldbronyboy ⊠ 22 points · 11 months ago
ACAB
⊟ **Reply Share Report Save**

> **thinblueline__45** ⊠ -2 points · 11 months ago
> she's not even talking about cops, she's talking about
> private prisons, you dunce
> ⊟ **Reply Share Report Save**

>> **nastywednesday** ⊠ 17 points · 11 months ago
>> if you don't realize cops are an integral part of the
>> prison-industrial complex then I don't know what
>> to tell you, my guy
>> ⊟ **Reply Share Report Save**

>> **staygoldbronyboy** ⊠ 7 points · 11 months ago
>> knew id get this comment as a response before i
>> even posted. should start playing
>> the lotto.
>> ⊟ **Reply Share Report Save**

nastywednesday ⊗ 5 points · 11 months ago
you spent enough time on reddit you can accurately predict what the top 10 comments are going to be on any post, the replies to those comments, and the replies to those replies. it's honestly kind of exhausting.
⊟ **Reply Share Report Save**

> **eggwigglesworth** ⊗ 3 points · 11 months ago
> that's because reddits an echo chamber my guy.
> ⊟ **Reply Share Report Save**

> > **guycappsbot** ⊗ 0 points · 11 months ago
> > Which guy?
> > ⊟ **Reply Share Report Save**

> > > **eggwigglesworth** ⊗ 2 points · 11 months ago
> > > bad bot
> > > ⊟ **Reply Share Report Save**

> > **batmanbatmanbatman** ⊗ 2 points · 11 months ago
> > the internets an echo chamber dude. Its the same everywhere.
> > ⊟ **Reply Share Report Save**

> > **marksarcophagus** ⊗ 1 point · 11 months ago
> > echo chamber?
> > ⊟ **Reply Share Report Save**

> > > **staygoldbronyboy** ⊗ 1 point · 11 months ago
> > > echo chamber

⊡ **Reply Share Report Save**

eggwigglesworth ⊗1 point • 11 months ago
echo chamber . . .
⊡ **Reply Share Report Save**

marksarcophagus ⊗ 40 points • 11 months ago
Didn't she post one of these for David White?
⊡ **Reply Share Report Save**

batmanbatmanbatman ⊗ 14 points • 11 months ago
looking at her uploads, she did, and she posted it two days
before anyone knew he was missing. interesting . . .
⊡ **Reply Share Report Save**

eatabagofdicks_0_ ⊗ 2 points • 11 months ago
we're just letting death threats and advocating for violence go
unchecked now? . . . damn feminazi bullshit
⊡ **Reply Share Report Save**

40scoreand4bluntsago ⊗5 points • 11 months ago
anyone hungry all of a suddeN? i've never heard of andoulle but
i'm all bout chorizo and shit looks similar
⊡ **Reply Share Report Save**

PM_ME_PICS_OF_UR_FEET ⊗ -8 points • 11 months ago
show ur feet
⊡ **Reply Share Report Save**

[instagram.com]

⊠

samwachiknsammy ✓ · Follow ⠀⠀⠀⠀⠀ . . .

samwachiknsammy Here w/dozens of others protesting "Dirty Harry" Pendejo's tent prisons! CC imprisons so many asylum seekers on a daily basis they can't even house them all! Families and their children should not be subjected to this!

50w

bouncingbetty8402 keeping the filth off our streets. good on mr. cadejo.

50w⠀⠀⠀⠀⠀9 likes⠀⠀⠀⠀⠀Reply

givemealitreofcola Someone please explain to me how these are any different from concentration camps?

50w⠀⠀⠀⠀⠀15 likes⠀⠀⠀⠀⠀Reply
⸻⠀⠀⠀⠀⠀Hide Replies

> **dirtyharryver1fied** @givemealitreofcola THEY SHOULDNT HAVE BROKE THE LAW PRISONERS GET THROWN IN PRISONS GET OVER IT
>
> 50w⠀⠀4 likes⠀⠀Reply

luchadeerultra get harry on record talking about this . . . CC gets paid $700 per prisoner per day and they're living in tents? Where's that money going?

50w   2 likes   Reply

3,113 views
50w

[twitter.com]

Trending · #CCsdeathcamps · 2,445 tweets

Chad Preston @badhocwifi2077 · April 15

These are concentration camps, pure and simple. Come Correct has an obligation to make sure the asylum seekers they are illegally holding do not DIE IN THEIR CARE #CCsdeathcamps

---

5 Replies   3 Retweets   3 Likes

The Washington Post @washingtonpost · April 15

A combination of seasonally high temperatures, overcrowding, and a continuing drought leave 23 dead in Come Correct's "temporary" prison tents in Texas (washingtonpost.com)

---

30 Replies   42 Retweets   85 Likes

Quarter Pound Royale @hamberderswcheese · April 15

Come Correct has a contract with the US government for private prisons . . . so why are CIVILIANS being kept in TENTS in 90 degree heat w/o air conditioning?
INHUMANE!!! #CCsdeathcamps

---

2 Replies   1 Retweets   4 Likes

AK 1776 @redhatakimbo · April 15

Typical libtards . . . NOT EVERYONE YOU DON'T LIKE
IS HITLER!! If they didn't want to be in prisons THEY
SHOULDN'T HAVE BROKEN THE LAW!!!
#CCsdeathcamps

31 Replies   4 Retweets   8 Likes

The Meme Economy @memeeconomyrec · April 15

DO YOU LIKE POSTING MEMES WELL NOTICE ME
SENPAI GET PAID FOR POSTING MEMES HECK YOU'RE
DOING IT ANYWAY KEK
#CCsdeathcamps #memes #BillHR23201 #lol #anime
#videogames #SenatorBilbin #NevadaNun #MisfitCircus
#Caturday #MakeAmericaMemeAgain

3 Replies   Retweet   2 Likes

Grace S. @graceofgod558630 · April 15

Praying for the prisoners in Texas. They're criminals, but that
doesn't mean they deserve to die for their sins. They deserve
humane conditions!
#CCsdeathcamps

Reply   **2 Retweets**   **1 Like**

[facebook.com]

Posts

PROTECT THE AMERICAN DREAM PROTEST
April 20 at 5:45 PM

Remember, this is a PEACEFUL PROTEST! Let's not give
any ammunition to the critics who say opposers of Harry's
concentration camps support violence against Americans!
UNDER NO CIRCUMSTANCES DO WE CONDONE
VIOLENCE AGAINST THE COUNTER PROTESTORS!
Remember to bring water, it's supposed to be a hot one!

471 likes   155 Comments   415 Shares

Like   Comment   Share

PROTECT THE AMERICAN DREAM PROTEST
April 19 at 1:48 PM

MARK YOUR CALENDARS!! On Saturday, April 23rd we
will be protesting at Harry Cadejo's ranch in Beeville, Texas to
show the world that we do not condone his illegal detention of
families seeking asylum in the GREATEST COUNTRY IN THE
WORLD, THE UNITED STATES OF AMERICA! Bring plenty
of water to beat the heat!
Bring first aid kits, food, and water to make the protests as safe as
possible! Spread the word!

834 Likes   105 Comments   229 Shares

Like   Comment   Share

PROTECT THE AMERICAN DREAM PROTEST
April 16 at 3:00 PM

America was built by immigrants. The inscription on the Statue of Liberty says "Give me your tired, your hungry, your poor . . ." In illegally detaining FAMILIES trying to make a better life for themselves, CC is destroying the American Dream itself. On April 23th we will protesting at Harry Cadejo's ranch in Beeville, Texas to demonstrate to him that REAL Americans don't approve of hisconcentration camps!

901 Likes   60 Comments   415 Shares

Like   Comment   Share

[reddit.com]

▲ 53 ▼

r/texas · Posted by u/demsarefubar ⊗ 11 months ago

Counter Protest Scheduled at Harry Cadejo's ranch in Beeville

We need to show these snowflakes that we will not be silenced, we
will not be made a minority in our own country, and that we will
not tolerate CRIMINALS being sent over our border en masse to
steal our jobs, our tax dollars, and our very lives. Start showing
up at 9AM. Exercise your 2A rights but make it clear that we will
NOT make the first move. Unprovoked violence shows the MSM
that we are just as bad as the vermin they defend. Harry Cadejo is
a g-ddam DEFENDER of American values and we will not let the
leftists intimidate him— come and show your support!

SORT BY **CONTROVERSIAL** ▼

utriggeredyet ⊗ 17 points · 11 months ago
protecting the american dream? what a joke. its called the
AMERICAN dream not the mEXICAN dream checkmate leftists
⊟ **Reply Share Report Save**

+Comment removed by moderator (0 children)

+gottachutemall -20 points 11 months ago

+Comment removed by moderator (0 children)

tednugentscrossbow ⊗ 25 points · 11 months ago

gonna be there BRIGHT AND EARLY with my LEGALLY
PURCHASED RIFLE. Would love for sum libs to try to take it
away from me. JUST TRY

⊟ **Reply Share Report Save**

+Comment removed by moderator

aocmorelikebbc ⊠ -4 points • 11 months ago
isn't showing up with guns asking for trouble? even if they're
legal and all the paperwork . . . wouldn't be surprised if deep
state agents show up and use the coutner protests as an excuse to
"confiscate" (IE steal) our guns. or for the MSM to paint us as
militia or asking for trouble . . .

EDIT: downvotes? really? for logic? ok . . .

⊟ **Reply Share Report Save**

+Comment removed by moderator

(Show more comments)

[twitter.com]

Trending · #PTADprotest · 2,866 tweets

Grace S. @graceofgod558630 · April 23

Would be attending the #PTADprotest if I could take off
work . . . Jesus was an immigrant. The israelites were immigrants.
Hebrews 13:2 and Malachi 3:5 tell us to welcome refugees with
open arms . . ..

Reply   **3 Retweets**   **3 Likes**

Riley Frank @he11odoktornik · April 23

Have plenty of water for everybody at the
#PTADprotest. Table is stationed at the south side near the sign
table. Counter protestors too! No heat stroke for anyone today!
#fingerscrossed

8 Replies   **18 Retweets**   **20 Likes**

REALREALTY @cashgashmoney · April 23

Make REAL CASH MONEY $$$ selling homes from the
comfort and privacy of YOUR home!! CLCIK SEE REAL
TESTIMONAILS FROM REAL PEOPLE NOT ACTORS!!
#PTADprotest #PTADprotest #PTADprotest
#PTADprotest #PTADprotest #PTADprotests

Reply   Retweet   9 Likes

GLITTERPINK @gpstreams247 · April 23
Replying to **@tiffanysesqr**

OMG . . . are they for real? i'd get out of there rq . . . couldn't pay
me to share space with actual nazis . . . stay safe tiff! And everyone
else at #PTADprotest!!

17 Replies   14 Retweets   36 Likes

AK 1776 @redhatakimbo · April 23
Replying to **@tiffanysesqr**

You mean fifteen AMERICANS exercising their 1A and 2A
rights????? y would you fear for yr life unless your a threat
yrself!?!??! #PTADprotest

30 Replies   11 Retweets   21 Likes

Tiffany Soldat @tiffanysesqr · April 23
Replying to **@tiffanysesqr**

3rd group of counter protestors I've seen with rifles . . . fifteen
total? Four wearing Iron Cross patches, one w/ actual swastika.
First time I've protested where I've actually feared for my life.
#PTADprotest

28 Replies   **12 Retweets**   **30 Likes**

[twitch.tv]

STREAM CHAT

2:25:16 **sparkleshun**: more people there than i expected

2:25:20 **BinchItsMe**: seems like more protestors than counter protestors

2:25:30 **squirrelindrag**: crazy to me that so many people there have guns, is that legal in America?

2:25:42 **firecrotchgacha**: 2A baybee, hell yeah it's legal here

2:25:57 **gokuplusultra**: does that guy wit hthe riot shield have an SS patch on his arm?

2:26:07 **BinchItsMe**: wild

2:26:11 **uncle_johnny_v4**: goku, looks like it, doesn't it?

2:26:15 **BinchItsMe**: WILD

2:26:18 **spiderpigspiderpig**: if i lived in America i'd never leave the house

2:26:26 **firecrotchgacha**: shootings are rarer than the media would have you believe

2:26:30 **sparkleshun**: jennifer, stay safe, you never know what will set these incels off

2:26:42 **firecrotchgacha**: think of how big the country is, and the frequency of shootings

2:26:51 **wyatthunk23**: paid protestors, SAD

2:27:05 **firecrotchgacha**: why are they incels? cuz they're exercising their 2A rights? fuck off

2:27:10 **wyatthunk23**: why do all the protestors signs look the same? thinkaboutit

2:27:20 **BinchItsMe**: they're incels cuz they're cosplaying fucking nazis, dude

2:27:26 **MandyMob4447**: anyone have the name of the girl with the pink hair w/jen?

2:27:30 **LaserLasagna**: i can tell they're incells by their faces, bro

2:27:34 **wyatthunk23**: SAD

2:27:45 **CRIMsonCARson**: typical leftists, thinks gun ownership makes you a nazi

2:27:48 **CRIMsonCARson**: fuck off

2:27:52 **BinchItsMe**: THEY'RE WEARING LITERAL SS PATCHES

2:28:00: **sparkleshun**: was that a gunshot?

2:28:01 **uncle_johnny_v4**: is someone shootig?

2:28:05 **gokuplusultra**: aw fuck, here we go

2:28:06 **sparkleshun**: WAS THAT A GUNSHOT?

2:28:08 **spiderpigspiderpig**: HOLY SHIT

2:28:11 **MandyMob4447**: anyone have the name of the girl with the pink hair w/jen?

2:28:13 **BinchItsMe**: HOLY SHIT

2:28:15 **LaserLasagna**: RUN

2:28:16 **BinchItsMe**: HOYL SHIT

2:28:20 **firecrotchgacha**: RUN BITCH RUN XD

2:28:23 **spiderpigspiderpig**: this is so fucked up

2:28:24 **sparkleshun**: JEN WHAT ARE YOU DOING STOP TRYING TO STREAM

2:28:26 **CRIMsonCARson**: calm down, no ones actually shooting, those don't even sound like gunshots

2:28:29 **BinchItsMe**: this is america smh

2:28:31 **squirrelindrag**: the stream go down for anyone else?

2:28:35 **sparkleshun**: HOLY FUCK JEN ARE YOU OKAY?

2:28:40 **MandyMob4447**: anyone have the name of the girl with the pink hair w/jen?

2:28:45 **LaserLasagna**: sparkle, yeah, it's dark

2:28:50 **sparkleshun**: fuck fuck fuck i hope everyone's okay :((((

[twitter.com]

Trending · #PTADshooting · 2,866 tweets

The New York Times @nytimes · **April 24**

12 injured in Beeville, Texas after shots ring out during anti-private prison protests at Harry Cadejo's ranch (nytimes.com)

---

13 Replies   24 Retweets   40 Likes

Grace S. @graceofgod558630 · **April 24**

Thoughts and prayers for those hurt in the #PTADprotest . . . no one should be hurt or threatened for fighting for their fellow man #PTADshooting

---

Reply   Retweet   3 Likes

Caturday Knight @cattycassandrea · **April 24**
Replying to **@nytimes**

MISLEADING HEADLINE! 12 were injured in the ensuring RIOT, not because of GUNS . . . shots WERE fired but NO ONE WAS SHOT PROTESTORS attacked COUNTER-PROTESTORS LOOK IT UP #PTADshooting

---

16 Replies   5 Retweets   10 Likes

Eric The Bard @ericericboberic · **April 24**
Replying to **@nytimes**

def a false flag op . . . if you watch that jen girl's stream there's
over thirty shots fired from two different guns but not a SINGLE
PERSON was shot??? Someone WANTED to start a riot
#PTADshooting

Reply   **Retweet**   **1 Like**

AK 1776 @redhatakimbo · **April 24**

whos pushing this hashtag??? why is it #PTADshooting and not
PTADriots? No one was shot!!! Not a single person!!! Guns didn't
do this, LIBS DID!!!

19 Replies   **4 Retweets**   **Likes**

[reddit.com]

▲ **338** ▼

r/conspiracy · Posted by u/rainbowchemtrails___ ⊗ 11 months ago

Youtube vigilante killing and eating the rich

reddit user u/ashwhateverr posts a video on r/videos explaining how she killed David White and made tacos out of his tongue on 2/10 > David White misses his Dawn of the Rising Sun show in New Orleans on 2/13 and hasn't been seen since (excuse is that he's sick, but that's bullshit, it's been months) > u/ashwhateverr posts a video on r/videos explaining how she killed Harry Cadejo and turned him into sausage on 4/3 > protests occur at Cadejo's ranch on 4/23, shooting occurs > Cadejo hasn't publicly addressed the shooting two weeks later, hasn't been seen in public since 4/1 (no excuse given, estate is not even addressing his disappearance)

Who's next?

SORT BY **BEST** ▼

tedcruzisbtk ⊗ 86 points · 11 months ago
You're not even going to link the video? Cite your sources, man.
⊡ **Reply Share Report Save**

> **rainbowchemtrails___** ⊗ 118 points · 11 months ago
> sorry, click **here** for her youtube channel
> ⊡ **Reply Share Report Save**

bibleofanunnaki ⊠ 94 points · 11 months ago
ty man, dates check out, this is wild if true
⊡ **Reply Share Report Save**

clintondeathcount ⊠ 5 points · 11 months ago
https://lmgtfy.com/?q=reddit+user+ashwhateverr
⊡ **Reply Share Report Save**

tsarbomba911 ⊠ 33 points · 11 months ago
hey asshole, it's not crazy to ask for citations in the post itself, make it easier for everyone to follow the story.
⊡ **Reply Share Report Save**

MKMichelobUltra ⊠ 72 points · 11 months ago
dates line up too evenly to be a coincidence. this shit is CRAZY, how is no one in the MSM talking about this? Good on Ash, it's BEEN time to eat the rich
⊡ **Reply Share Report Save**

PM_ME_UR_FURS0NA ⊠ 50 points · 11 months ago
Like batman but in reverse. I dig it.
⊡ **Reply Share Report Save**

daddyspuddin229910 ⊠ 1 point · 11 months ago
fuckin furries besmirching batmans good name smh
⊡ **Reply Share Report Save**

PM_ME_UR_FURS0NA ⊠ 35 points · 11 months ago
Bruce Wayne is a billionaire who, instead of using his wealth to help Gotham through philanthropic means, or by paying his fcking taxes, chooses to dress up as a bat to beat Gotham's mentally ill and

poor into submission. Imagine if Lawson Rich dressed up in a Halloween costume and went around beating up homeless people in NY. Batman is a psychopath.

⮐ **Reply Share Report Save**

> **sandrasohface** ⌧ 28 points • 11 months ago
> Never thought I'd agree with a furry on the ethical and moral ramifications of Batman's methods, but I guess here we are.
>
> ⮐ **Reply Share Report Save**

pickleriiiiiiiiiiiiiiiicky ⌧ 23 points • 11 months ago
Eat the Rich is a philosophy, it's not supposed to be literal. We should be breaking up monopolies, taxing the 1% the way we did in the 50s, supporting unions and holding these mfers accountable for destroying the environment . . . redistributing the wealth . . . not literally killing and eating them. Fing gross.

⮐ **Reply Share Report Save**

> **rainbowchemtrails___** ⌧ 65 points • 11 months ago
> So how's the weather in dreamland? In the hypothetical place where everything that "should" happen, does? Because in the real world, the weather is shit. The planet's literally on fucking fire and if we don't scare these shitheads into doing the right thing it's never going to happen.
>
> ⮐ **Reply Share Report Save**

daddyspuddin229910 ⌧ 42 points • 11 months ago
Yeah, we SHOULD have been doing those things all along, that's the way things should have been for the last twenty, thirty, fifty years, but none of that shit's happening and the entire time enlightened centrists like yourself have been preaching about the way things

"should" be done, the rich have been bleeding the planet dry and fucking the poor to death. Fuck the way things "should" be done, it's time for radical thinking. Ash has got the right idea. EAT THE RICH!!

⊟ **Reply Share Report Save**

(Show more comments)

Episode 3

Rocky Mountain Oysters

DO YOU THINK this is a joke? That's fine. Do you think this is an art piece, some kind of satire expected to prove a point? Heck no, that's where I draw the line. I've been many things in my life: a movie theater usher, a cashier, a waitress, but I've never been an artist. I don't get it. I've never been a creative, which might explain the editing and production values on these videos. I'm just a working-class woman who's sick and tired. That's all. Above all, I'm hungry. So it's time to eat.

The balls in front of me belonged to Rocco "Rocky" Mann, the CEO of pharmaceutical company Citizen One. At the time of his death, Rocco Mann's net worth was one hundred and forty million dollars.

Now, if you're some kind of leftist, centrist, conservative wage slave lackey who's so blinded by the false promises of capitalism that you feel the need to defend the people whose boots are perpetually on your neck, you might say, "Ash, liquid assets aren't the same as net worth, Rocco didn't *literally* have one hundred and forty million dollars in the bank; it's all in the company!" Well, yeah, duh, I know how money works. But that's not the point. Rocco lived in a McMansion and had a yacht and two summer homes and a private jet and the reason he was afforded these luxuries is because he preyed on the sick. The weak. He exploited peoples' basic needs and human rights to the point where people died and he did so to increase his company's profits. So the difference between net worth and liquid assets is negligible. Rocco Mann was rich and he made his riches by denying people healthcare and medicine. So tonight I'm frying the man's balls.

Like "Dirty" Harry Cadejo, Rocco definitely gave himself the nickname "Rocky," but I'm not complaining. The copy practically writes itself. Tonight we're making Rocky Mountain oysters, aka cowboy caviar, aka swinging beef, aka cattle fries, aka dusted nuts, aka Montana Tendergroins (relevant considering Rocco was born in Montana). If you're not aware, Rocky Mountain oysters aren't shellfish at all—they're testicles. I cut off Rocco's balls and I did it when he was awake, for flavor. I didn't need to, but I did. The recipe I'm using calls for two pounds of bull testicles instead of two old man balls, so a lot of the ingredients for the breading might go to waste; consider purchasing actual bull testicles so you can see what Rocky Mountain oysters are actually supposed to taste like. Or fry some other stuff, I don't know. Just throw some stuff in the fryer. Your mileage may vary.

To make Rocky Mountain oysters, you're going to need the following:

- 1 tablespoon salt
- ½ cup flour
- ½ tablespoon vinegar
- ¼ cup cornmeal
- 1 cup red wine
- Salt & pepper
- Garlic powder

On a side note that's not really a side note, the opioid epidemic continues full swing. In 2019, over fifty thousand people died as a result of an opioid overdose, and while that number includes drugs like heroin and fentanyl, it also includes prescription painkillers. Including the deaths from heroin in that statistic is a part of my argument, and not an attempt to bolster the numbers: according to the National Institute on Drug Abuse, 80 percent of people who use heroin first misused prescription opioids. America's reliance on opioid prescriptions, on opioid use for pain management, and how expensive prescription drugs are directly contributes to creating American heroin addicts and overdose deaths.

And no, I didn't mention that apropos of nothing. Citizen One makes, and aggressively markets, a potent opioid painkiller called Numres. You may have seen commercials for Numres on your TV, and if that doesn't seem strange to you, consider that the United States is one of only two countries in the world that allows pharmaceutical advertising directly to consumers (the other is New Zealand, strangely enough). Rocco's company, Citizen One, flooded the airwaves with commercials peddling their addictive drug, telling patients to "ask your doctor about what Numres can do for you."

And if that doesn't bother you, if your argument is that it isn't illegal so it must be moral, then turn the video off now. I'll get back to Numres, back to Rocco Mann and his sins, but first we need to get his balls ready to fry.

There's a tough outer exterior surrounding the balls, like a skin. Split it and peel each of them. You can use a knife for this. Be careful; cut away from your hand. You don't want to spill your own blood. Soak the balls in salt water for an hour, then drain. Fill another pot with enough water to cover the balls, then add the vinegar and parboil. Drain. Rinse.

Let the balls cool. You don't want to burn yourself. You don't know a lot about cooking but you know cutting or burning yourself is not part of the process. Slice Rocco's testicles into quarter-inch thick slabs. The meat is tougher than you think and it takes more effort than you'd expect, but it'll be worth it. Sprinkle the salt and pepper on both sides for taste.

In 2015, Rocco Mann was charged with and found guilty of orchestrating a criminal conspiracy to bribe doctors to prescribe Numres to patients. Patients that didn't need it. He employed sales reps that "persuaded" doctors to boost prescriptions to the medication. He bribed insurance companies to make sure the medication was covered. He lobbied senators to keep Marijuana a Schedule II drug, the same schedule as opioids, funnily enough, so that patients couldn't access nonaddictive pain relief. He spent more on marketing the drug than he did the drug itself.

Rocco Mann was sentenced to thirty three months in jail, which was substantially less time than the thirteen years the prosecutors pushed for. He was sent to some country club prison where rich people go and released after twenty months for good behavior. I don't have to link to specific cases; people without Rocco's means get sentenced to jail for life for selling marijuana and marijuana possession all the time. If I have to explain to you why this is unfair, well, you haven't been paying attention.

Combine the cornmeal, the flour, and the garlic to taste. Roll each of the ball slabs in the mixture. Dip them into milk. Roll them again in the flour mixture. Dip them into the wine. Roll them again in the flour mixture. Repeat if you want a thicker crust. I recommend it. The less ball taste, the better. You're going to eat Rocco Mann's balls, but that doesn't mean you have to like the taste. Better to mask the flavor.

Citizen One doesn't just sell Numres. They sell a whole host of other medicine, including insulin and their proprietary epinephrine injector, Epiject. Insulin helps people with diabetes manage their blood sugar levels; epinephrine is a drug that narrows blood vessels and opens airways in the lungs. It's most commonly used for people with nut allergies once they've been exposed to nuts, but can be used for other forms of anaphylaxis.

A year's supply of insulin costs Citizen One around fifty dollars to make. For someone without insurance, insulin can cost more than a thousand dollars out of pocket per *month*. Epinephrine injectors cost a few dollars to make; Citizen One charges a thousand dollars for a pack of two. This may sound normal to you since you've been submerged in our communal capitalist hellhole your whole life, but it is not. I repeat: just because it's legal doesn't mean it's moral. These are lifesaving medicines that people need to survive, and Citizen One price gouges the people who need them because they're a captive audience. They could charge far less and still make a healthy profit.

Americans have started to ration their insulin or turn to crowdfunding sites like Backer to be able to afford it; people have died because of rationing insulin or because they lack the money to buy insulin at all. At least thirty people have died in the last three years due to insulin rationing. Those deaths are on the hands of Citizen One and every company like them.

To fry the balls of this old, out-of-touch capitalist pig, you'll need the following equipment and ingredients (note: there are many ways to fry food at home, but I chose the easiest method with the tools I had available):

- A large, deep pot with high sides
- A kitchen spider or a wire basket
- Pair of long, metal tongs
- A crap ton of paper towels
- A frying thermometer
- Canola oil

Fill the pot with canola oil. Not all the way. Make sure there is enough in the pot to fully submerge the balls slabs, but leave a few inches between the top of the oil and the top of the pan to prevent it from boiling over. Place the pot on the stovetop, making sure the area is clear of other objects. Heat the oil to around 375 degrees Fahrenheit. Use the frying thermometer for accuracy. The temperature is important.

Use the kitchen spider or wire basket to lower the ball slabs into the oil. You don't want to just plop them in there; that's just asking to get burnt. Don't fry too much at once. If you overcrowd the pan, the temperature of the oil could drop, and you'll get heavy, greasy balls. While the meat fries, use metal tongs to flip the slabs, making sure to evenly cook the outside to ensure the inside gets evenly cooked as well. You don't want to eat raw ball meat, trust me.

You're going to want to fry the slabs until they're a golden brown. Use the kitchen spider or wire basket to remove the slabs from the oil, then place them on a paper towel to dry. Slap some hot sauce on them bad boys. You could eat them with cocktail sauce too, but hot sauce might make the oysters more . . . palatable. You're not optimistic about the taste. What you've made doesn't look that appetizing.

Citizen One isn't just a threat to Americans, they're an international threat as well. In 2016, documents leaked from a whistleblower in Citizen One's research division that highlighted deaths in nations abroad due to Citizen One conducting homebrew medical trials. Twelve people died in Uganda in 2012 due to previously untested Alzheimer's medicine. Three sets of people were tested: a control group that received a placebo, a group that received a consistent daily dose of the medicine, and a group that received the medicine intermittently. Everyone in the third group died within eight weeks. Their families were not paid out because none of them finished the trial, a stipulation in the contracts the deceased signed that none of them understood because the contracts were in English, and none of them were bilingual or were provided translations in their native tongue.

Fifteen people died in an unnamed southern Indian village in 2014 due to a previously untested variant stem cell treatment for muscular atrophy. All of the people that died were homeless, some of them were illiterate— none of them knew the risks of the treatment they were subjected to. These "volunteers" were at least provided contracts in their native language (Tamil), but after their deaths Citizen One realized that the contracts were terribly translated, so much so that none of the "volunteers" even knew what they were being treated for, let alone the risks. Citizen One couldn't even be bothered to pay actual, reputable translators for their contracts. Because of the high rate of illiteracy with the subjects, most of them were read the contracts by their "doctors"— none of these people were actual doctors. They were paid actors wearing white lab coats that paraphrased the already poorly written contracts and fifteen people died as a result.

These are not the only incidents. I have briefly described two of the six known documents. They're all heinous; they're all flat-out *murder* due to negligence and malice and exploitation, but they're all very similar to one another. Citizen One preyed on the weak, on the poor, to test their medicine and people died. No one went to jail for these crimes. They were barely talked about in the media. Citizen One quietly closed their research division in 2017, six months after the documents leaked.

When asked about the research division's closure in an earnings call,

Citizen One's CFO Guy Capps responded by saying, "Curing patients is not a sustainable business model." He didn't mention the whistleblower, he didn't mention the leaked documents, and he certainly didn't eulogize the dead. The dead that were only dead because of Citizen One. He invoked Citizen One's bottom line, and he did so in a way that encapsulates the American healthcare system in a nutshell.

Eat Rocco's mountain oysters. They taste . . . terrible. There's a reason they use calf testicles when they make for real Rocky Mountain oysters, and that's because the meat's much more tender. Rocco's balls are tough. God, they're tough. The texture . . . the fried, crispy exterior and the hot sauce do nothing to hide the texture. You gag with the balls in your mouth. But you eat them regardless. That part doesn't matter so much—the eating itself. The more important part is that it is eaten.

Chew the meat that used to be Rocco Mann and turn it into paste. Swallow it and digest it with your bile. Then crap him out. Ashes to ashes. Dust to dust. Human crap to literal crap. That's what he deserves, what he was always meant to be. Rocco Mann's millions can't help him now.

Eat the rich. It never was a metaphor. They just hadn't pushed us far enough yet. It's been too long since the last revolution. Let's start a new one. Let's turn platitudes into reality; let's turn a toothless mantra into a mouth that churns. Let's make them shake in their boots and regret their words and deeds.

If you liked this recipe, consider going to Backer and donating to campaigns that haven't met their goals. Find someone who can't afford their medicine, that might suffer or die without it, and help in any way you can. Recognize that Backer is a symptom of late-stage capitalism, that people shouldn't *have* to go online and beg strangers for money to survive, but also realize that until we can fix America's healthcare system, until we can hold the leeches and the fat pigs accountable, there are still people out there who need help. Help in any way you can.

Until next time, stay hungry.

[reddit.com]

▲ **405** ▼

r/conspiracy · Posted by u/MKMichelobUltra ⊗ 10 months ago

NEW EAT THE RICH VIDEO

Video's been posted on Ash's **youtube**, but hasn't been posted to reddit yet. Subscribed to her channel after the last vid and I just got the notification. If you're not following the story, **u/rainbowchemtrails___** posted a **pretty good summary** a while ago. LSS: Redditor ashwhateverr uploaded videos claiming that she killed David White and Harry Cadejo and cooked and ate them. Turned David's tongue into *Tacos de Lengua* and Harry into *Andouille*. Each video was uploaded days before they were known to be missing. Just uploaded a new video saying that she killed Citizen One CEO Rocco Mann and cooked his balls a la rocky mountain oysters.

This is the turning point, yeah? This is the thing that either proves the whole thing real or proves it to be a coincidence. If it's fake: I dig the message of the videos and their production value is better than Ash gives herself credit for. If it's real: holy shit, this is fucking bananas, all three of them deserved to die and this might be the beginning of an actual movement.

SORT BY **BEST** ▼

illuminattyice ⊗ 131 points · 10 months ago
anyone else notice something wonky with her face?

⊡ **Reply Share Report Save**

cocainemountains ⊠ 22 points · 10 months ago
love that on any video a female posts, the top comment is
someone shaming their looks.
GTFO with that shit
⊡ **Reply Share Report Save**

illuminattyice ⊠ 94 points · 10 months ago
that's not what i meant, dipshit. there's weird
artifacting on her face throughout the vid and she
looks ten years older than she did the last time she
posted. was wondering if maybe she was doing
some digital manipulation bullshit to hide her
identity
⊡ **Reply Share Report Save**

15bearswithguns ⊠ 11 points · 10 months ago
Yeah I noticed that too, was wondering if maybe this was
a deep fake and not what she actually looks like
⊡ **Reply Share Report Save**

15bearswithguns ⊠ 0 points · 10 months ago
Yeah I noticed that too, was wondering if maybe this was
a deep fake and not what she actually looks like
⊡ **Reply Share Report Save**

15bearswithguns ⊠ -5 points · 10 months ago
Yeah I noticed that too, was wondering if maybe this was
a deep fake and not what she
actually looks like
⊡ **Reply Share Report Save**

jesusfckaioli ⊠ 95 points · 10 months ago

Interesting how she doesn't mention CO pushing Somagolix, a dangerous untested drug, for NOVA-90 treatment near the beginning of the crisis. Eight people DIED because of CO's investment in the drug and they never mentioned it again as soon as news of those deaths came out.
⊟ **Reply Share Report Save**

> **peggreflast** ⊠ 59 points · 10 months ago
> Might be because Guy was the one on television pushing Somagalix. It wasn't really a CO or even a Mann thing. The first time Mann mentioned Samogolix in public was him saying it still needed to be tested before we whole hog committed to it as a cure.
> ⊟ **Reply Share Report Save**

>> **guycappsbot** ⊠ 22 points · 10 months ago
>> Which guy?
>> ⊟ **Reply Share Report Save**

>>> **peggreflast** ⊠ 13 points · 10 months ago
>>> Guy Capps, he works at CO . . .
>>> Edit: nvm, looked at the username. got me, bot.
>>> ⊟ **Reply Share Report Save**

> **gliiixafor** ⊠ 31 points · 10 months ago
> After the Cadejo video, I was wondering why she kept bringing up NOVA-90 . . . maybe she knows someone that died from it, and its personal? And maybe she didnt bring it up here bcuz she didnt want to make it too obvious and give away hints at her identity.
> ⊟ **Reply Share Report Save**

>> **jesusfckaioli** ⊠27 points · 10 months ago
>> Maybe she brought up NOVA-90 because it was a

recent, global crisis that many rich people used to
line their pockets to the detriment of the popu-
lace at large? I don't care why she left it out, it's
criminal she doesn't mention it here. CO lied and
people died.
⊟ **Reply Share Report Save**

bombXglossy ⊠ 67 points · 10 months ago
I'm worried that by actually killing and eating the rich, she's
perverting the message she's trying to spread. Do we really want to
associate anti-capitalism with murder and cannibalism? It'll make
it that much easier for the other side to demonize us and call us
all murderers and cannibals. I hope for all of our sakes that this is
a satirical art piece and not a cookbook for snuff film aficionados.
⊟ **Reply Share Report Save**

> **PauperPlacebo** ⊠ 23 points · 10 months ago
> They do that anyway. They call us leeches and rats and
> insist that they earned their money while all we want is
> handouts and shit for free. If they're going to deny us our
> humanity anyway, then we might as well be what they all
> assume we are.
> ⊟ **Reply Share Report Save**

SCPFaccountant ⊠ 49 points · 10 months ago
def using a deepfake to hide her identity, which is smart. only
hope that she did it from the beginning and the first video doesn't
show her real face, or she's bout to get suicided real quick
⊟ **Reply Share Report Save**

> **snrcaptaincoff33** ⊠ 20 points · 10 months ago
> this just in, "ashwhateverr" found in a studio apartment
> with the door busted open by battering ram. she died by
> two gunshots to the back of the head. her apartment had

been scrubbed clean with bleach. her death is being ruled a suicide.

⊡ **Reply Share Report Save**

> **mangovikingfuneral** ⊠ 19 points · 10 months ago
> She somehow stuffed her own dead body into a duffel bag and locked it from the outside. She shot herself eighteen times from a distance of ten feet and then dumped the duffel bag into a river. No foul play is suspected. The remains were accidentally scheduled for cremation and the ashes were launched into the sun.
> ⊡ **Reply Share Report Save**

>> **aliensgonnahenge** ⊠ 11 points · 10 months ago
>> She sniped herself in the head from a distance of 1.2 miles and then scheduled her apartment complex for implosion thirty minutes later. Every cop assigned to her case was promoted out of the department and given a hundred thousand dollars for just being really good cops. Authorities say it was an open and shut case and the cops are to be commended for their hard work.
>> ⊡ **Reply Share Report Save**

commacommallama ⊠ 35 points · 10 months ago
This runs deeper than just predatory pricing. All these pharmaceutical companies are dosing their drugs with female hormones, increasing the rate of homosexuality and transgenderism in America and further perpetuating the LGBTQ agenda (citation **here**). Not only that but CO is dosing the water supply with mind-numbing agents that make people more "tolerant" to the lesser races and less likely to fight back when

the outsiders finally invade (citation **here**). Masculinity is under attack. Whiteness is under attack. It's a dangerous time to be a white male in America. Arm yourselves, people.

🖅 **Reply Share Report Save**

> **bombXglossy** ⊠ 85 points · 10 months ago
> People are actually upvoting this garbage? Remember when r/conspiracy wasn't filled with racist, homophobic bullshit? Pepperidge Farm remembers.
> 🖅 **Reply Share Report Save**

>> **mangovikingfuneral** ⊠ 75 points · 10 months ago
>> Check comma's post history. They're part of the subreddit that must not be named, and when they make a post like the one above they link to it in that quarantined shithole and all their members come and upvote it. It's a way of making their views seem more mainstream than they actually are. Just downvote them and don't reply, don't give them the satisfaction of "triggering the snowflakes".
>> 🖅 **Reply Share Report Save**

>> **15bearswithguns** ⊠ 32 points · 10 months ago
>> r/Conspiracy has always been filled with racists. Not a knock against the subreddit, it just comes with the territory. Not all conspiracy theorists are racists, but you better believe that most racists are conspiracy theorists. Everything is the fault of the jews, the fault of the blacks, the fault of whites who believe in equality, everything. It's always been that way. Best to ignore them and don't give them the satisfaction.

⊡ **Reply Share Report Save**

(Show more comments)

[reddit.com]

▲ 566 ▼

r/videos · Posted by u/ashwhateverr ⊠ 10 months ago

EAT THE RICH EPISODE 3 - Rocky Mountain Oysters
youtube.com/watch? . . .⌐

SORT BY **BEST** ▼

CPDeckrNET ⊠ 214 points · 10 months ago
As a mother of two sons, both of which are allergic to peanuts,
this really hit home. EVERY place that they spend any amount of
time at needs to have epijects, just in case, and they expire every
year. You can only buy them in two packs, and each child needs
their own two pack for some reason. Their school needs epijects.
Their babysitter needs epijects. Their after school care needs
epijects. Their summer camp needs epijects. Both me and their
father need epijects on us, just in case, and there needs to be some
at home as well. THOUSANDS AND THOUSANDS of dollars
every year just to make sure my sons don't DIE . . . I always knew
there was a mark up, but it only costs them a few dollars to make
each one? And I spend a fifth of my salary every year on the damn
things? It's criminal.
⊡ **Reply Share Report Save**

> **byebyekitty5008** ⊠ 15 points · 10 months ago
> It's not about the cost to produce, it's about the cost to
> research the product, make sure it works and doesn't
> accidentally kill the user, it's about the cost of facilities
> and staff and everything that goes into the company. CO

is a company first and foremost and the cost to produce their products isn't the only cost they incur. You're basically saying that your sons aren't worth the price to keep them alive. You're a bad mother and you should feel bad.

⊟ **Reply Share Report Save**

> **jennifersomebody** ⊠ 29 points · 10 months ago
> Oh fuck off, dude. How's that CO dick taste? Like the video says, Mann's net worth ALONE is 140 mil, that's not even scratching how much CO is worth. Kids are going to die because they're parents can't afford the fuckin things. There's literally no reason they need to charge so much, other than they're ufckin evil
>
> ⊟ **Reply Share Report Save**

>> **byebyekitty5008** ⊠ 12 points · 10 months ago
>> How many kids have died because their parents couldn't afford epijects?
>> Can you link to any reputable sources (i.e. not fake news) of even a SINGLE child dying? I can wait.
>>
>> ⊟ **Reply Share Report Save**

>> **CPDeckrNET** ⊠ 170 points · 10 months ago
>> How fucking DARE you! Of course I love my kids!! That's why I buy the damn things in the first place!! I bet you don't fucking have kids . . . every dollar I spend on epijects is less money I have to buy them food and toys and other shit to make their lives better. That money is going to CO instead of my kids and you have the GALL to say I'm not a good mother because I complain about the price? FOH plz

68 |

🗗 **Reply Share Report Save**

fractalzncreme ⊠ 112 points • 10 months ago
Pro-tip, you can use them even if they're expired. I make
20K a year and with rent, food, car insurance, couldn't
afford to buy one when mine expired last year. But I read
that they last longer than the expiration date so I'm just
holding onto the old one.
🗗 **Reply Share Report Save**

> **CPDeckrNET** ⊠ 77 points • 10 months ago
> Thanks, but the school/aftercare/summer camp
> won't accept expired epijects. They just flatout won't
> take in my kids if they don't have new ones every
> year.
> 🗗 **Reply Share Report Save**

> **byebyekitty5008** ⊠ 3 points • 10 months ago
> Get a better job. It's not CO's responsibility to
> make sure you have your precious epijects, their
> only responsibility is to their bottom line
> 🗗 **Reply Share Report Save**

> **jennifersomebody** ⊠ 40 points • 10 months ago
> You're really everywhere in this thread defending
> CO, huh? How much CO stock you have? Or are
> you some fifteen y/o incel and don't have any idea
> how the real world works? SAD bro
> 🗗 **Reply Share Report Save**

xxnarutosmokesbluntsxx420 ⊠ 95 points • 10 months ago
that's why you need to use calf testicle and not bull testicle, the
calf testicle is much more tender. If she was a real cook she'd
know this

▣ **Reply Share Report Save**

> **jennifersomebody** ⊗ 142 points • 10 months ago
> Did you even watch the video? Not only does she
> acknowledge that she's an amateur cook, but the whole
> premise of the video is that she's making rocky mountain
> oysters from an old man's balls. She's not going to kill a
> baby, she's not a monster.
> ▣ **Reply Share Report Save**
>
> > **subparcornoncob** ⊗ -2 points • 10 months ago
> > dems are baby killers anyway it'd be on brand

jennifersomebody ⊗ 65 points • 10 months ago
Made a subreddit at r/asheatstherich, join us if you want to follow
the story as it happens!
▣ **Reply Share Report Save**

(Show more comments)

[twitter.com]

Search · #AshEatstheRich · 3.1M tweets

Sienna Black @tortugablack227 · **May 8**

PLEASE let this shit be real . . . People been saying
EAT THE RICH for years on this hellsite but ASH out
here making it a REALITY!! #AshEatstheRich

---

7 Replies   **12 Retweets**   **20 Likes**

VVVVV. @namastevixen · **May 8**

Quand les pauvres n'auront plus rien à manger,
nous mangeons les riches!
- Michael Foucault

When the poor have nothing more to eat,
they will eat the rich.
-Translation

#AshEatsTheRich

Reply   Retweet   2
Likes

MEMES ALL DAY EVERY
@BuffaloWildMemes · **May 8**

TEENS REACT TO #ASHEATSTHERICH
VIDEO *GONE WRONG* (youtube.com)
#AshEatstheRich #eattherich #ashwhateverr
#memes #notclickbait

---

31 Replies   **55 Retweets**   **80 Likes**

Jack Washington @defnotarushnbot1779 · May 8

COMMUNIST SCUM ATTACKING AMERICAN
BUSSINESS OWNERS LITERAL DEMOCRAT
CANNIBALS HANG EM HANG EM ALL
#AshEatstheRich

---

1 Reply   **3 Retweets**   **112 Likes**

Art Everett @boomerandproud58 · May 8

#AshEatstheRich starting a youtube channel is the
Zoomer version of the Zodiac killer writing letters to
newspapers. All killers want is notoriety, and we
should not give it to her.

Reply   Retweet   1
Like

Melissa Misfit @missxdblxmisfit · May 8

Listen, I'm not gonna shed any tears for the white dead billionaires.. But I'm also not gonna stan a murderer and a cannibal. Are y'all the people who read Silence of the Lambs and thought Hannibal was the good guy? #AshEatstheRich

---

6 Replies   **24 Retweets**   **20 Likes**

Caturday Knight @cattycassandrea · May 8

false flag op, fr . . . david white, harry cadejo, and rocco mann, they're all safe and sound in the CARRIBEAN with their money while everyone THINKS they're dead . . . just another way to hold onto their billions . . . #AshEatstheRich

---

Reply   **3 Retweets**   **7 Likes**

Caturday Knight @lasagna____bear · May 8

#AshEatstheRich really wants to get caught, huh? Putting out a video per kill using her own face. Taking bets on whether it's the FBI or the incels on 4CHAN that find her first . . .

---

11 Replies   **20 Retweets**   **22 Likes**

[becomeabacker.com]

BACKER♥

HELP BETTY BAKER FIGHT BREAST CANCER

$22,148 raised of $10,000 goal
(DONATE NOW / SHARE)

Tiffany Baker is organizing this fundraiser on behalf of Betty Baker.

Created April 28, 2021 | Medical, Illness & Healing

On April 9th, my mother Betty Baker was diagnosed with stage 2 breast cancer. After consulting with her doctor the doctor decided the best course of treatment was a mastectomy. Fortunately, they found it early enough that she doesn't need chemotherapy or radiation therapy. My mother hasn't worked in some time, choosing instead to raise me and my siblings (which in itself is one of the hardest jobs there is), and while my father's job's insurance covers her, EVEN WITH THE INSURANCE the cost for a mastectomy can run upwards of $10,000. The hit to our savings would bankrupt the family, so to help alleviate some of the costs we've come to Backer to appeal to the kindness of strangers. EVERY LITTLE BIT HELPS! My mother is the sweetest, most inspiring woman I've ever met, and she refuses to have the procedure done if it means it'll bankrupt the family. She's a proud woman, so she never would have made this page herself— but pride is less important than her life. Please consider helping to keep my mother in my life. AGAIN, EVERY DOLLAR HELPS! THANK YOU AND GOD BLESS!! <333

Updates (3)

May 3, 2022
by Tiffany Baker, Organizer

$1,000 raised in less than a week! Thank you so much for your support! Thank you to the fifty people who donated and remember, every little bit helps!

May 5, 2022
by Tiffany Baker, Organizer

We've hit $2,000! This is incredible! I never could have imagined! My mom found out about this Backer page and while she initially was upset that I would "beg the internet for money," she burst into tears when she saw how many kind people there are out there that would help a stranger in need! One fifth of the way there!

May 10, 2022
by Tiffany Baker, Organizer

I AM IN TEARS . . . I NEVER COULD HAVE DREAMED
WE WOULD HIT $20K!! I DON'T UNDERSTAND HOW
WE WENT FROM 80 DONATORS TO OVER SEVEN
HUNDRED BUT I'VE LEARNED NEVER TO QUESTION
THE WILL OF GOD! THANK YOU! YOU'VE SAVED MY
MOTHER'S LIFE!!!!!

Donations (801)

Cheryl Delgado
$50 · 1d

Ben & Lisa Novack
$30 · 1d

Anonymous
$20 · 1d

Tracy Drang
$50 · 1d

Anonymous
$10 · 1d

Comments (2)

Ben & Lisa Novak donated **$30**

Praying for the family

1d

Jennifer Somebody donated **$50**

Ash sent me #EattheRichFeedthePoor

1d

[reddit.com]

▲ **299** ▼

r/conspiracy · Posted by u/MKMichelobUltra ⊠ 10 months ago

4chan in the process of doxxing Ashwhateverr

Screenshotting **available threads** because no one should have to go to that hellsite.

/Pol/ has decided that Ash is a deep state operative whose purpose is to dismantle American democracy and capitalism and has gone all in on attempting to dox her. In the process it looks like they doxxed some random woman not even connected to ETR, swatting her and getting her fired from her job. Real despicable shit.

Regardless of whether or not you believe the ETR vids are true (I think there's substantial evidence to prove they might be), doxxing Ash WILL result in her death. If the videos are real: the govt will assassinate her, as any threat to the m/billionaire class is a threat to the oligarchy and thus the American govt itself. If the videos are fake: some lone wolf y'all qaeda operative will hunt her down as soon as her real identity is published. I'm sharing this here because it's worth knowing how far the billionaire bootlickers will go to defend their oppressors.

CONTENT WARNING FOR IMAGE: literally everything. Racist, homophobic, sexist slurs. Encouraging suicide, depictions of violence. Don't click if you're squeamish.

SORT BY **BEST** ▼

View all comments

jetfuelcantmeltmemes ⊠ 127 points · 10 months ago
Transcription of the images in case you can't get to IMGUR:
(Reiterating OP's CW, some of this shit is gross, I'll censor the
worst stuff)

(Screenshot 1)
[Screenshot of Ash's face from ETR1] OP: Illuminati k***s send
deep state communist assassin against TRUE AMERICAN
HEROES who dared achieve the AMERICAN DREAM. ThEY
ARE THE TRUE ROT AND CANCER THAT WILL EAT
AWAY AT &nd ERODE THE TRUE AMERICA
Y'all know what we need to do
DOX DOX DOX DOX DOX DOX ERRBODY

1: Easy stuff first, outlet in the back shows she's American,
accent is hard to place but isn't southern or mid eastern, maybe
east coast. Brand names for all the ingredients are available
nationwide, so nothing there. First name is likely Ashley, or a
derivative, last name might be a red herring but might also sound
or rhyme with the word whatever. Searching k***book and twatter
and instawhore for other accounts with that username don't come
up with anything, but I did find a livejournal (of all things) from
2012. It's private, though maybe we can brute force the pass.

2: deep state or not, i'd fuck her ass

3: obv using some sort of deepfake tech for the third video to
make herself look older, but wondering if that's maybe a red
herring as well??? why use a deepfake only to make herself look
older when she posted the orig vids with her real face—thinking

maybe she used deepfake tech for all three vids but made it looks sloppy on the third one to throw us off the scent

4: if she's hungry, i'd just chop off her tits and feed them to her. problem solved, she looks like a t****y anyways

5: looks like a race traitor from my hometown. name's not ash tho, it's jamie ******. she's too dumbfuck to be deep state but heard her spout SJW prop on more than one occasion, maybe getting filled with n***** cum all day warped her brain and now she's ISIS

6: is this the livejournal you were talking about? livejournal. com/~xxxxxxxxx

7: can someone make out the take out flyers on the kitchen counter in the background?

8: any bitch that's eatin old man balls is crazy AF, i'm not fuckin w/her

9: yeah, that's the LJ i was talking about. got locked out after 3 wrong pass attempts but now i'm going through her friends trying to find any info on location

8: @7, ENHANCE, ENHANCE, ENHANCE

this isn't CSI that shit doesn't work in real life

resolution/angle isn't good enough to make out the flyers, i already tried

9: jamie ******? this jamie ******? facebook.com/xxxxxxx? could be . . .

🖂 **Reply Share Report Save**

jetfuelcantmeltmemes ⊠ 113 points · 10 months ago

(Screenshot 2)
[Screenshot of Ash's face from ETR2] OP: ash's
livejournal:
livejournal.com/~xxxxxxxxx

only solid lead atm

let's find this bitch anon, make her pay

1: three of her LJ friends are public, reading through their
backposts now trying to see if they're RL friends or just
people she knew from LJ. will keep anon updated

2: anyone get any hits off the AIM username listed in
the LJ info? i downloaded AIM and friended her, but
obviously shes offline. googling to see if she has any other
accounts with the username "danslesabysses"

3: phone number and address for jamie ******: [not
posting this for obvious reasons]

4: called jamie's cell phone and home, letting that bitch's
fam know what their daughter is up to

5: jamie ******'s work number, seems like she works for
citizen one? is that why she went after mann? either way,
let's spam their phone lines and get this bitch fired

6: JAMIES CURRENTLY STREAMING AT THIS
LINK: twitch.tv/******** SWAT

SWAT SWAT SWAT

7: you guys got the wrong bitch, one of her lj friends mentions they went to a movie theater in poughkeepsie, ny, that jamie c*** lives in CT

8: found jamie's boyfriend on KB, this the n****r that you saw op? His name is paul *********. home address & phone#: [again, not posting this for obvious reasons]

9: IDC IF THIS THE WRONG CUMBUCKET ANON, WE'RE TOO FAR IN NOW. SWAT TEAMS ON THE WAY

10: made a bot that tweets "KILL YOURSELF" at jamie's twitter every three seconds, get it here github.com
⊡ **Reply Share Report Save**

> **jetfuelcantmeltmemes** ⊗ 105 points • 10 months ago
>
> (Screenshot 3)
> [Screenshot of Ash's face from ETR3] OP: got all we can get from ash's LJ AFAWK ash lives or used to live near poughkeepsie, ny jamie ****** is NOT ash repeat jamie ****** is NOT ash (not that we should regret ruining that race traitor's life) currently at a dead end, maybe the next vid will give more clues
>
> 1: still not convinced jamie isn't ash
>
> 2: if you guys had even checked her FB you would've seen jamie was out of the country at the

time david white was killed, you guys are normies
fr

3: she doesn't look anything like ash. You guys
went all "we did it reddit!" and doxxed the wrong
bitch

4: looks don't matter if shes deepfaking her face
you cuck

5: did you autists even watch the twitch stream?
She has a s*** accent you r***** fucks

6: LMAO at OP calling her a race traitor XD

7: doesn't matter, swatted a s***, today was a good
day

8: did we even consider HOW ash is kidnapping
and killing? She must have access to money, a
team . . . maybe we should follow the money . . .
try to find who's bankrolling her . . .
🗗 **Reply Share Report Save**

sandrasohface⊗ 28 points · 10 months ago
Jesus fucking christ, it's hard to believe this is how actual
human beings think and act.
🗗 **Reply Share Report Save**

> **rainbowchemtrails___** ⊗ 11 points · 10
> months ago
> What else do you expect from radicalized alt-right
> 14 year olds? This isn't even the worst part of the

internet, it's just the most easily accessible "back corner" there is.

🗔 **Reply Share Report Save**

> **benitorigatoni** ⊠ 8 points • 10 months ago
> Don't excuse their behavior, not all of them are kids. There are grown ass human beings that act and think this way too. Some of them are even people you know. They just don't say it out loud in mixed company because they know the shit they think is vile. The internet can be inspiring and can showcase the best humanity has to offer, but it can also be vile and a cesspool and showcase the worst. Two sides of the same coin.
>
> 🗔 **Reply Share Report Save**

shakethatbearrrrrr ⊠ 6 points • 10 months ago
What do you expect from a site that got popular because of child porn? Friend of mine in college recommended I try /b/ because of "memes" and when I went there the first thing I saw was CP . . . immediately called the police because I don't need that shit on my conscience

🗔 **Reply Share Report Save**

> **ezdiphthong** ⊠ -2 points • 10 months ago
> Says the guy whose username is based on a video of two people fucking on a bear they just shot and killed . . .
>
> 4Chan didn't get "famous" bc of CP, they got famous DESPITE it. Pedos were attracted to 4chan because of the anonymous nature of it but mods always took down CP as soon as they saw it. Don't lump in all of anon with those pedo fucks.

We kicked them out and then they went and
started 8chan, now THAT'S a cesspool.
🖃 **Reply Share Report Save**

rainbowchemtrails___ ⊠ 22 points • 10 months ago
Of course all the people in the image are disgusting human
beings, and the fact that they doxxed that poor girl is horrible,
but I do find one point (and only one point) that they made to
be valid . . . how is ash eating the rich in the first place? How
is she kidnapping and killing these high-profile people, these
millionaires that ostensibly have security? Is she government
backed, is she ex-military or part of some well-funded militia? Is
she backed by other millionaires harboring vendettas and taking
out rivals? Or is she rich herself? Not that that would invalidate
her cause, not exactly, but it's worth talking about.
🖃 **Reply Share Report Save**

[twitter.com]

Trending · #BackerBenefactors · 4,009 tweets

Aaron A. @archivistaaron6 · May 14
Replying to @archivistaaron6

I went to Backer after the price of my meds jumped from
$14 per pill to $750 overnight, never expecting more than a
hundred or two . . . BUT IT JUST HIT $12K!!! THANK YOU
#BACKERBENEFACTORS!! (3/3)

13 Replies   **21 Retweets**   **44 Likes**

Evie M. @bonsaibarbie99 · May 14

HOLY CRAP! THE BACKER FOR MY BABY BROTHER
JUST HIT $18K!!! HE'S GONNA BE ABLE TO HAVE THE
HEART SURGERY!!!
THANKS TO ALL THE #BACKERBENEFACTORS,
WHOEVER YOU ARE! <3333

3 Replies   **4 Retweets**   **19 Likes**

Sienna Black @tortugablack227 · May 14
Replying to @tortugablack227

. . .and NO ONE is giving #AshEatstheRich credit?
The media still isn't talking about ETR? What's with the

#ETRblackout? #BackerBenefactors

---

5 Replies   **7 Retweets**   **15 Likes**

Sienna Black @tortugablack227 · May 14

So let's get this straight . . . Ash puts out a video urging people
to donate to worthy Backer efforts, so many are funded that
#BackerBenefactors gets to trending, checking the comments of
the top Backer pages of the month shows hundreds of comments
saying
#Ashsentmehere . . .

---

5 Replies   **8 Retweets**   **24 Likes**

OBEY SALT BURN @obeysaltburn · May 14

Are we just not going to talk about the fact that we're the type of
society that NEEDS to have #BackerBenefactors? Like, we can't
even rely on our own government to take care of us, so we need
strangers to do it? Guess y'all not ready for that convo.

---

1 Reply   **Retweet**   **1 Like**

Brittany Has a Bazooka @bazookababe999 · May 14

I wouldn't normally do something like this, but seeing everyone
post their #BackerBenefactors stories: due to some unforeseen

expenses, I can't afford my hormones for this month. Please consider donating to my backer campaign!! (becomeabacker.com)

---

1 Reply   Retweet   1 Like

JJ Johnson @jockstrapjam223 · May 14
Replying to @ 11daft_monk11

Live within your means? What does that even mean in the context of medicine you need to survive or a medical emergency? You live in the UK, dude. Sit the fuck down.

---

4 Replies   2 Retweets   7 Likes

Random Excess Memories @11daft_monk11 · May 14

I don't need #BackerBenefactors because I live within my means and don't expect hard-working people to subsidize my lifestyle . . . #BackersareBeggars

---

15 Replies   2 Retweets   2 Likes

Welcome to Barkerville @bollojojo · May 14

I'm in tears right now . . . thanks to all the #BackerBenefactors we can buy enough insulin for my baby boy for more than a year! Their truly are good people out there!!!

4 Replies   **4 Retweets**   **5 Likes**

[instagram.com]

⊠

roccosthemann ✓ · Follow   . . .

roccosthemann Always wanted to visit Greece!
Love the way my hair looks in this video.

45w

funfrankfurter0 who follows a pharma ceo on insta?
Why does this even exist?

45w   5 likes Reply

kpopstanley Not even a good deepfake.
#ThatsNotRocco

45w   8 likes   Reply
———   Hide Replies

> **liliesonparade** @kpopstanley I've seen better
> deepfakes in tutorial videos on youtube.
> You'd think CO would be able to do better
>
> 45w   5 likes   Reply

teapainauto55 hair looks really good for a dead guy

45w   Reply

j4bbathebutt audio is sampled from other videos

ON HIS INSTA . . . do they really think we're that stupid? #ThatsNotRocco

45w   Reply

shivlaffmuff lovin' all the replies, people are finally opening their eyes . . . #EATTHERICH #THATSNOTROCCO

45w   Reply

7,926 views
45w

Episode 3.5

Channel Update

THERE IS NOTHING wrong with your computer monitor. Do not attempt to adjust the picture. I am still Ash, despite what your eyes and ears tell you is real. My face looks different, but I am still the same Ash you've come to know over the past few months. That face was never mine; it was always a simulacrum. My voice sounds different, but you've never heard my real voice. It was always an amalgamation of all the voices silenced by those I've eaten. My house looks different, but it was never really my house to begin with. It was always a set.

Let me explain.

You've made subreddits, you've made hashtags, you've made posts and comments lauding and condemning what I've done. But you do not know me. Not exactly, anyway. You know people like me. You are a person like me. I am you and you are me and we are we and we are all together. But you do not know *Ash*.

Some people have speculated that my face has been deepfaked, but that isn't true. It's a good guess considering what you know about the world, but there is another world beneath the one you know. The fact that my face isn't being deepfaked doesn't matter. I am using technology that I've acquired to hide my identity, and that's all you need to know. I've acquired it illegally from the sort of people that we talk about when we say we need to eat the rich. You can try to find me but you won't. Your technology doesn't compare to theirs. Maybe *they* can find me . . . but until then, I'll take out as many of them as I can.

The reason I'm breaking the fourth wall is because the rich are doing everything they can to keep the truth from you. Sally White has taken David's mantle and still claims her husband is sick and/or recovering from an unexplained illness. Harry Cadejo's estate refuses to acknowledge his death and claims he's in hiding due to threats from you, the hungry. Citizen One put out a deepfaked video of Rocco Mann that claims he's alive and well and on vacation abroad. This is not true. You know it, they know it, but they need to present a reality that denies everything we're trying to accomplish here. The veneer is thin but holding. What we need to do is break it. That's what I'm trying to do here.

We need to talk about the media. The media is lying to you. It sounds like your classic basic bitch conspiracy theory but it's true. Oh, the not cursing thing was an affect. Sorry for the deceit. Anyway. Your favorite pundits, regardless of station or affiliation, are puppets and mouthpieces for the rich and they won't talk about us because they're scared of us. They'd rather pit us against one another than highlight the fact that together, we're stronger than them. They'd rather stoke fear and foment hatred among us than allow us to realize that our true enemy is those who would squish us under their heel. The ones who hoard their paper and numbers that represent millions of hours of underpaid labor while people starve and freeze to death and stab each other in the streets over scraps. Fuck those people. I've killed three of them, and I hope to kill and consume dozens more.

People have questioned where I get the resources for these videos. And that's a valid question. I'm not David White, or Harry Cadejo, or Rocco Mann. I haven't made my wealth exploiting and bleeding and leeching from the working class and the sick and the oppressed. I stole from them and used their money against them. That's the only way we win. That's the only way to beat them. Use their money, which they stole from you, to get back at them.

So we get to the crux of this video. We can eat the rich, but we cannot make them fear us until they know that they are being eaten. I had originally saved the bodies for another purpose. But to expose what we are doing here, everyone needs to see what we have done.

I have made it somewhat of a game. A treasure hunt. It's not an issue of entertainment. The reasons are threefold. One, the more people we have looking for the eaten, the bigger the splash will be when they are found. Two, if you are the ones to find the bodies, the less chance there is that the authorities will cover it all up. Livestream your progress. Three, to cover my tracks. By the time you find the bodies, I will be long gone.

Call the number on your screen to get the first clue. Maybe you'll be the one to find David, Harry, and Rocco. Maybe you'll be the one to find their bodies. Maybe you'll be the one to find a hundred thousand dollars of David White's money strapped to his chest.

Once you find them, make a video naming your favorite charity and I'll match the 100K in donations using Harry's and Rocco's money.

In the meantime, I'm planning something big. No need to like or subscribe. If I succeed, you'll hear about it.

Until next time. Stay hungry.

[discord.com]

#WIN-DAVID-WHITES-MONEY

Slaphappy 05/26/2022
Where's everybody at

Traffic 05/26/2022
williamsport memorial library

Traffic 05/26/2022
but no idea where to go from here

Slaphappy 05/26/2022
Wait, did I miss something? What happened after the wayback machine

Andru 05/26/2022
keep up, slap

Andru 05/26/2022
we're way past that

Slaphappy 05/26/2022
I had to go to work numbnuts

Slaphappy 05/26/2022
I can't just quit my job to find this fcker

Traffic 05/26/2022
LOL there's other hunters here, hi guys

Layla 05/26/2022
You think all the clues are going to be in DC or

Traffic 05/26/2022
is everybody else just wandering around looking @ random books, or just me

Andru 05/26/2022
wait you're done with work already

Slaphappy 05/26/2022
Nah Im AT work I wanted to check in

Jennifer 05/26/2022
stay on topic guys

Jennifer 05/26/2022
traffic, you're the one that actually found the library card, right?

Jennifer 05/26/2022
the pics you took were really low res, any way yo ucan scan them?

Jennifer 05/26/2022
I can't even read the name on the card

Slaphappy 05/26/2022
Whatd I miss?

Layla 05/26/2022
I'd like to be part of the hunt but I live in Colorado u.u

Andru 05/26/2022
Watt used the wayback machine to find some lifestyle blog from the early 2000s or some shit

Andru 05/26/2022

and the only pics on the page were of that persons trip to the chesapeake
& ohio canal national historical park in MD

Fisk 05/26/2022
@Layla, you can still help! People all over are finding clues who aren't
able to join the physical part of the hunt. Watt earlier was the one who
found the wayback machine clue, which was crucial

Jennifer 05/26/2022
traffic? you see my chat?

Andru 05/26/2022
Watt lives in Wyoming but traffic lives like an hour drive from the park
so traffic took off work and went to the spot where the picture was taken

Slaphappy 05/26/2022
Wild, this whole thing is wild

Andru 05/26/2022
They found a library card for the williamsport memorial library in a plas-
tic baggie in the CANAL with a signed note from ash egging them on

Andru 05/26/2022
So traffic went to the library and now we're trying to find the next clue

Jennifer 05/26/2022
traffic, if you're gonna be our man on the ground you gotta stay in
touch bud

Traffic 05/26/2022
The name on the card is 'HI TARTY WAYLEAVES'

Fisk 05/26/2022
LOL

Andru 05/26/2022
WTF?

Jennifer 05/26/2022
Maybe an anagram for an author?

Andru 05/26/2022
Maybe just a red herring

Andru 05/26/2022
Remember the audio in the background of the voicemail, turned out to be nothing

Layla 05/26/2022
ASHLEY is part of those letters . . . maybe it's an anagram for her real name!?? O.O

Traffic 05/26/2022
You guys really gotta stop sharing clues outside the discord, there's like fifteen other people here who are obviously part of the hunt

Traffic 05/26/2022
If we're not the ones who find the bodies then we're not gonna be able to split the pot

Jennifer 05/26/2022
We're not gonna be able to find them by ourselves. This is bigger than all of us, traffic

Jennifer 05/26/2022
I live in NY first of all

Jennifer 05/26/2022

Also it's not like you're the only one who's found clues, we've used info we found elsewhere too

Andru 05/26/2022
idk, seems kinda tongue in cheek to me, i think it's a red herring

Andru 05/26/2022
Maybe we should be checking out anti-capitalist lit? Marx, chomsky, etc?

Jennifer 05/26/2022
Lol, is that your go-to? You should read more, Andru

Traffic 05/26/2022
That's the first place everybody else went, if that's where we're supposed to go, it's covered

Layla 05/26/2022
Brb guys i'm gonna go check out the subreddit and some other discord servers i'm a part of, maybe they figured something out

Traffic 05/26/2022
Lemme know, I'm just standing ehre with my dick in my hands

Fisk 05/26/2022
What charity are you going to choose if you're the one who finds 'em, traffic

Andru 05/26/2022
I'd go child's play, it's a charity that buys video games for kids in hospitals

Fisk 05/26/2022
That's nice. Makes their lives a little bit easier

Jennifer 05/26/2022
ACLU, mostly based on ash's rec

Slaphappy 05/26/2022
LRAN for me

Traffic 05/26/2022
Trevor Project

Traffic 05/26/2022
My sister's trans and she killed herself three years ago cuz she didn't get the support she deserved

Fisk 05/26/2022
Sorry to hear that. :/ but nice that you'd do that for her memory

Chris 05/26/2022
Youre brothers a fucking fag

Chris 05/26/2022
Dead fucking faggot

Fisk 05/26/2022
The fuck dude

Andru 05/26/2022
Who even are you?

Jennifer#xxxx banned **Chris#xxxx**
05/26/2022
With reason: shithead

Andru 05/26/2022
Who even was that?

Jennifer 05/26/2022
idk, the servers public. Sorry about that

Andru 05/26/2022
Not your fault

Traffic 05/26/2022
Fuck

Fisk 05/26/2022
Don't let it get to you dude

Traffic 05/26/2022
I'm done here idk wtf I'm even doing

Andru 05/26/2022
Probably a follower of white or some shit

Fisk 05/26/2022
Okay traffic . . . take care of yourself man.

Jennifer 05/26/2022
Donating $10 to the trevor project in that assholes name just to spite him <3

Traffic 05/26/2022
ty guys, i'm gonna get some food. ttyl

Layla 05/26/2022
GUYS they found the next clue

Layla 05/26/2022
Looks like the blackwater national wildlife refuge

Layla 05/26/2022
You up for a little more driving, traffic?

Layla 05/26/2022
Traffic?

[facebook.com]

Posts

PRAYERS FOR DAVID WHITE
May 24 at 7:49 PM

Followers, these so called "treasure hunters" are sinners and deceivers of the highest degree. David White is NOT dead. Sally has told us as such! If you know of any so called "treasure hunters" in your life, please educate them to the truth and donate to #thechurchofwhite in their name so their sins may be forgiven! "A false witness will not go unpunished, And he who breathes out lies will perish. - Proverbs 19:9"

367 likes   47 Comments   99 Shares

Like   Comment   Share

PRAYERS FOR DAVID WHITE
May 18 at 1:19 PM

Followers of White, it is much more serious than we previously thought. News came out today that Sally and David have had to sell their yacht to cover medical costs incurred by David's illness (whatever that may be). That is UNACCEPTABLE! What has the White family ever done to deserve this? Have the followers of White not been seeding their faith adequately? WE NEED YOUR DONATIONS, FOLLOWERS! PLEASE HELP CORRECT THIS TRAVESTY AND RESTORE THE WHITE YACHT TO ITS PROPER OWNERS!!!

951 Likes   152 Comments   230 Shares

Like   Comment   Share

PRAYERS FOR DAVID WHITE
May 15 at 9:59AM

IT IS NECESSARY FOR YOU TO SHARE AND LIKE THIS
POST!!! SALLY WHITE HAS POSTED ON THE CHURCH
OF WHITE WEBSITE THAT THEY ARE $50,000 SHORT
OF DAVIDS NEXT TREATMENT AND THEY NEED IT
WITHIN THE NEXT THREE DAYS!!
SEED YOUR FAITH FOLLOWERS OF WHITE!!! I GAVE
THEM THE RECOMMENDED TITHE OF 10% OF MY
PAYCHECK AND THEN GAVE 10% MORE!!!
DAVID NEEDS YOUR SEED SO HE CAN FLOWER!!!
SHARE AND LIKE, WHITES!

2,209 Likes   358 Comments   639 Shares

Like   Comment   Share

PRAYERS FOR DAVID WHITE
May 12 at 5:45 PM

Sally White has cancelled the weekly #RisingSunTogether show
for the second week in a row. Her announcement: "It is with a
heavy heart that I must once again cancel the RST sermon this
week. David's health has taken a turn for the worse and I feel as

though spending time with him in his ailing health is what God would want. Please keep David in your prayers." Well put, Sally. Through God all things are possible. Let's show David how much we care.

Please consider donating to #thechurchofwhite and make sure to share and like this post.

Share/Like = 1 prayer!!!

810 Likes   83 Comments   476 Shares

Like   Comment   Share

[newsbyconews.com]

Harry Cadejo refuses to comply with House subpoena and doesn't show up for testimony regarding his "tent cities"
By Madeiline Wright | NEWSBYCO
Updated 11:08 AM ET, Wed June 2, 2022

(NEWSBYCO) — CEO of Come Correct Harry Cadejo refused to comply with the House's subpoena for testimony on Monday, citing the "illegal nature" of the subpoena.

Come Correct is the largest owner of private prisons and detention centers in the United States, and as the CEO Harry Cadejo has recently come under fire for the "tent cities" Come Correct has erected in response to the immigrant crisis on the border. After the deaths of several . . ..
Read more . . .

You need a subscription to continue reading this article. Covering the news and helping citizens stay informed costs money. For journalists, for staff, for server costs, etc. Please support NEWSBYCO in order to stay informed.

Keep reading for $50 $5

Cancel any time. Seriously. If at any time you don't feel informed, or don't support our mission, you can cancel your support (as dictated by US law).

More Offers | Already a subscriber? **Sign in.**

Sponsored Stories You may like   Ad Content by Barabos

— Sell Your Unused Diabetic Test Strips For $$$!

— You Won't Believe What These 25 Child Stars Look Like Now! (#19 BLEW OUR MINDS!)

— Is Your Boyfriend Cheating On You? If He Does These 5 things, Probably!

— 7 Tips For Talking To The Police When You Haven't Done Anything Wrong! Don't Get Caught In A Perjury Trap!

— 10 Tips For A Successful Backer Campaign That You'd Never Guess!

Get in on the Conversation! (4,017)

CAMULVANEY 10m
Don't break the law. It's that simple.
Reply • Share • Report

BethfullaGrace 10m
They're coming over here regardless because these TENT CITIES are better than the sh*tholes they left! THEY NEED TO BE WORSE, NOT BETTER!
Reply • Share • Report

MaPonderosa 11m
So, he's gonna get arrested, right? Because if he isn't, we just admit that if you're rich, you get to break the law. If I don't show

up for a court date, I get a warrant out for my arrest. But if you don't show up to CONGRESS to testify about how you made LITERAL CONCENTRATION CAMPS these liberals just furrow their brows and say "well, we tried"? How is that justice?
Reply • Share • Report

Rykers 11m
Good. Listen, I have nothing against immigrants. But they need to come over the RIGHT WAY. Not by breaking the law. Throw 'em in jail, and if we don't have room, throw 'em in tents. Deport them every time they try. America is for Americans.
Reply • Share • Report

BetterRedThanDead 11m
I DON"T SEE THE PROBLEM, THEY"RE CRIMINALS!!
Reply • Share • Report

OliverPearson 11m
The alien who resides with you shall be to you as the citizen among you; you shall love the alien as yourself, for you were aliens in the land of Egypt: I am the Lord your God.
Leviticus 19:34
Reply • Share • Report

TracyRearden 12m
Obviously, the tent cities aren't supposed to be permanent. If the prisons are full, what else is Mr. Cadejo supposed to do? Just let them go? Let them infiltrate America and suck up our tax dollars and take our jobs? Honestly I think the problem is with how long deportation is taking. If we sent them back more quickly, then the prisons wouldn't be full. Ask Congress about that.
Reply • Share • Report

SHOW MORE COMMENTS . . .

[twitch.tv]

STREAM CHAT

10:15:19 **KEKFEST**: the nite vision cam is so cool

10:15:24 **KEKFEST**: makes it look like swat team footage or sumthn

10:15:28 **RickRavioli**: is the forest still even open? ispeeps allowed to be there?

10:15:36 **QUOTETW33T**: it's a forest numbnuts, it doesn't close

10:15:43 **metalgearStalin**: it's not a forest it's a wildlife refuge

10:15:44 **AmishAliceNN**: google says the blackwater national wildlife refuge closes at 4PM

10:15:52 **RickRavioli**: be safe peeps, don't get in trouble -_-'

10:15:55 **QUOTETW33T**: did you even go to school

10:16:01 **QUOTETW33T**: a bunch of trees is called a forest

10:16:05 **QUOTETW33T**: there's no door, it doesn't close

10:16:12 **AmishAliceNN**: i mean he's technically trespassing

10:16:17 **AmishAliceNN**: in an attempt to find the carcasses of murder victims

10:16:18 **KEKFEST**: what brand nitevision goggles arey ou using peeps

10:16:27 **KEKFEST**: and how are you streaming from the goggles

10:16:30 **L9_Savannah**: uptime?

10:16:39 **BasedWalmartKid**: like 3 hours

10:16:44 **QUOTETW33T**: you don't stream from nightvision goggles kek

10:16:51 **QUOTETW33T**: it's probably just a setting on their cam

10:17:00 **BasedWalmartKid**: so hes just wandering around in the dark?

10:17:06 **shartski11**: prolly

10:17:13 **AmishAliceNN**: so like whats the chance that the bodies are actually here
10:17:15 **AmishAliceNN**: whats everybody think
10:17:20 **bellENDbucko**: pretty high, i think
10:17:24 **of_EDELVEISS0**: nonexistent, i just want to see him fall into a hole
10:17:28 **TR4SHBABY**: i mean that's where the clue led right
10:17:33 **TR4SHBABY**: that's what the subreddit said
10:17:40 **KEKFEST**: so like if i wanted to buy actual nitevision goggles where would i go
10:17:40 **RuntPunksUK**: reddit is cancer
10:17:46 **AmishAliceNN**: idk theres just too many coincidences for this to be a hoax
10:17:50 **AmishAliceNN**: i think
10:17:58 **shartskil1**: alice if youre amish how are you on twitch
10:18:07 **TR4SHBABY**: anyone else have like four tabs open watching different streams
10:18:11 **AmishAliceNN**: grew up amish, never went back after rumspringa
10:18:14 **TR4SHBABY**: im getting confused who is who they all have night vision on their cams XD
10:18:15 **KEKFEST**: is it legal to own nitevision goggles
10:18:17 **L9_Savannah**: casual, i have SIX streams open
10:18:26 **L9_Savannah**: if someone finds that cash shits gonna turn into hunger games real quick
10:18:31 **shartskil1**: kek are you accidentally typing your questions into chat instead of google?
10:18:31 **KEKFEST**: do nitevision goggles run on batteries
10:18:35 **shartskil1**: lol
10:18:39 **bellENDbucko**: hunters livestreaming the hunt are dumb af
10:18:45 **bellENDbucko**: police, FBI, CIA, they're all trying to find those bodies too

10:18:54 **RickRavioli**: has peeps said what charity he's gonna pick if he's the one who finds them
10:18:59 **kpopSLAPS**: st judes i think
10:19:01 **L9_Savannah**: hope peeps finds em then
10:19:08 **L9_Savannah**: i am actively rooting against Lyss right now because she said she'd donate to Wishes4Kids network
10:19:16 **RuntPunksUK**: why is Wishes4Kids bad
10:19:22 **L9_Savannah**: they've been embezzling donations for years
10:19:23 **bellENDbucko**: fuckin scam charity is what it is
10:19:27 **bellENDbucko**: preying on peoples goodwill and pocketing the difference since 1997
10:19:27 **KEKFEST**: how much do nitevision goggles cost
10:19:32 **AmishAliceNN**: kek, youre KILLING me XD
10:19:35 **shartski11**: https://lmgtfy.com/?q=everything+you+need+to+know+about+night+vision+goggles
10:19:39 **BasedWalmartKid**: wrex said he'd choose save america now if he finds the bodies
10:19:44 **BasedWalmartKid**: do these people totally miss the point of ashs videos or what
10:19:50 **of_EDELVEISS0**: isnt that that religious nutwing operation
10:19:56 **kpopSLAPS**: yeah they oppose abortion and homosexual marriage
10:20:01 **L9_Savannah**: they're only in it for the money, not the cause
10:20:05 **QUOTETW33T**: is ash like obligated to donate to those causes if the hunters choose them?
10:20:07 **KEKFEST**: thanks shart
10:20:10 **metalgearStalin**: quote think about what you're saying
10:20:13 **RuntPunksUK**: yes, i think. she said so anyway
10:20:19 **QUOTETW33T**: ???
10:20:22 **L9_Savannah**: ash is a radical left-wing serial

killer who's killed three millionaires already and EATEN
THEIR FLESH
10:20:26 **L9_Savannah**: do you really think she'd donate 100K to
save america now?
10:20:32 **RuntPunksUK**: yeah but she said she would
10:20:35 **bellENDbucko**: oh sweet baby boy
10:20:38 **RuntPunksUK**: are you saying she's a liar?
10:20:40 **L9_Savannah**: she wouldn't compromise her ideals
like that
10:20:41 **KEKFEST**: best night vision goggles for price
10:20:46 **RuntPunksUK**: let's agree to disagree
10:20:49 **shartski11**: KEK IS THIS A BIT OR WHAT
10:20:53 **L9_Savannah**: there is no agreeing to disagree about it,
your wrong
10:20:55 **BasedWalmartKid**: WAIT WAIT WAIT PEEPS
GO BACK
10:20:58 **RuntPunksUK**: youre*
10:21:00 **AmishAliceNN**: DID YOU GUYS SEE THAT?
10:21:02 **TR4SHBABY**: am i just imagining things or did y'all
see those bodies hanging from trees
10:21:02 **L9_Savannah**: well technically it's "you're" but just
attack my grammar when you don't have an arguement why
don'tcha
10:21:04 **RickRavioli**: someone tell peeps he walked right by the
freakin bodies
10:21:08 **BasedWalmartKid**: PEEPS YOU JUST WALKED
BY 100K
10:21:09 **bellENDbucko**: LOOK @ THE CHAT PEEPS
10:21:10 **RuntPunksUK**: argument* don't you?*
10:21:11 **shartski11**: THIS IS IT BOYS, EAT THE
RICH CONFIRMED
10:21:12 **L9_Savannah**: THE REVOLUTION STARTS HER
10:21:12 **kpopSLAPS**: PEEEEPS GO BACK THEY'RE
HANGING FROM THE TREES

10:21:13 **TR4SHBABY**: do y'all hear sirens?

10:21:15 **AmishAliceNN**: WAIT WHAT i went to the bathroom for two mins what'd i miss

10:21:17 **RickRavioli**: ARE THOSE SEARCHLIGHTS?

10:21:19 **QUOTETW33T**: is that a fucking helicopter

10:21:20 **L9_Savannah**: DID THE STREAM GO DARK FOR ANYONE ELSE?????

10:21:23 **AmishAliceNN**: STREAM IS DOWN

10:21:25 **bellENDbucko**: told you guys i fucking TOLD YOU GUYS

10:21:27 **RickRavioli**: STREAM WENT DOWN HOLY CRAP

10:21:28 **RuntPunksUK**: here*

10:21:30 **L9_Savannah**: HELICOPTER ON WREX'S STREAM TOO HOLY SHIT

10:21:32 **bellENDbucko**: THEY'RE TRYING TO COVER IT UP

10:21:33 **AmishAliceNN**: i can't believe this shit

10:21:35 **bellENDbucko**: THE WHOLE THING'S BEING LIVE STREAMED PIGS

10:21:35 **TR4SHBABY**: THERES TOO MANY HUNTERS STREAMINGTHEY CANT SILENCE THEM ALL

10:21:37 **L9_Savannah**: WREXS STREAM DOWN TOO

10:21:38 **AmishAliceNN**: theyre not ev en trying to hide it shit

10:21:40 **KEKFEST**: bought a pair of nitevision goggles thanks for all the help guys

[reddit.com]

▲ **4,191** ▼

r/asheatstherich · Posted by u/billionaireburger ⊗ 10 months ago

It's been TEN HOURS

Ten hours ago, twitch streamer PEEPS found the bodies of David White, Harry Cadejo, and Rocco Mann in the blackwater national wildlife refuge in MD at around 10:20PM. Within thirty seconds, his stream went down. Before the stream went dark, his chat heard sirens, a helicopter, and saw searchlights. Seven other hunters were livestreaming in the BNWR, two of which were close enough to also hear sirens and see the search lights. Their streams went dark as well.

It has now been TEN HOURS, and no reporting has been done on this on the major news sites or broadcasts. NO ONE has heard from Peeps, Wrex, or Lyss, the streamers whose streams went dark. Not even THEIR FAMILIES. This is a MASSIVE coverup and the only way we'll overcome it is by massive protests. TIME IS PRECIOUS. The more time passes, the more time they'll have to create the cover story.

There's no "until next time" here, folks. The time is RIGHT NOW. EAT THE RICH.

SORT BY **BEST** ▼

tombsunderbaghdad ⊗ 994 points · 10 months ago

Calling for protests and general strikes is good and all, but the thing people never seem to think about is a lot of people *can't* take off work to protest and if they strike, employers have the power to retaliate. If I take off work I will not get paid for that time and I won't be able to eat this week. If I take off any "substantial" time off work to protest I *will* get fired and get kicked out of my apartment for not being able to pay my rent. I am therefore powerless to stop any injustices from happening because I'm a slave to my job.

That being said, fuck systemic oppression, eat the rich, etc.

⊟ **Reply Share Report Save**

> **slickerpunch** ⊠ 683 points · 10 months ago
> THIS IS A FEATURE OF CAPITALISM, NOT A BUG. By making you a wage slave, they make you powerless to exact any change and hold them accountable for their abuses of power. This is exactly why we need to eat the rich.
> What OP said. There isn't an "until next time". IT'S NOW.
> ⊟ **Reply Share Report Save**

> **billionaireburger** ⊠ 432 points · 10 months ago
> You're right, and I apologize. Protest if you're able, strike if you're able. If you're not, the very least you can do is push everywhere on social media for the three hunters to be released from police custody (if that's where they are, which I think is a safe assumption).
> That's the first step. Social media pressure exposes more potential protestors to the cause and (theoretically) increases the number of protestors. We just need to make a catchy hashtag first.
> ⊟ **Reply Share Report Save**

>> **slaphappytv**⊠ 102 points · 10 months ago
>> #FreetheHunters, or maybe #FreetheHunters3

(rhyming helps virality). Also, peeps twitch user-name is currently trending, we could always try to get "blackwater national wildlife refuge" trending, or maybe bring the #AshEatstheRich hashtag back. You know what, fuck it, let's do all of them. The more hashtags, the better.
⊡ **Reply Share Report Save**

sskipdigby ⊠ 12 points · 10 months ago
if you don't like it, get a better job
⊡ **Reply Share Report Save**

tombsunderbaghdad ⊠278 points · 10 months ago
Oh, get a job? Just get a job? Why don't I strap on my job helmet and squeeze into a job cannon and fire off into job land, where jobs grow on jobbies?
Edit: you know what,fuck that, this deserves an actual proper response. I'm not going to tell you what I actually do because I'm not interested in doxxing myself, but I have a Master's Degree. I work in an "entry level" position that requires six years of experience in a program that has only existed for five. I get paid hourly and they purposefully only schedule me for 29.5 hours a week so they don't have to give me benefits. I don't get PTO and I get three sick days a year (which is standard in my industry where I live). Comparable positions in other countries pay three times my salary plus benefits. It took me A YEAR of applying to jobs to get this one. And trust me, I'm spending time in my off hours, hours I should be resting my body and mind and indulging in hobbies, looking for a better job. But there's only so many hours in the day and so much energy I can exert before I burn out. My situation is the norm, not the exception. So fuck off with your "just get a better job".

⊡ **Reply Share Report Save**

> **PHDinBirdLaw** ⊠ 42 points · 10 months ago
> i get that reference
> ⊡ **Reply Share Report Save**

> **sskipdigby** ⊠ -2 points · 10 months ago
> if your position pays three times your salary in
> another country, just move to that country, prob-
> lem solved? but i guess youre not smart enough to
> figure that out, huh
> ⊡ **Reply Share Report Save**

> > **tombsunderbaghdad** ⊠ 98 points · 10 months
> > ago
> > Yeah, fuck me for wanting to live near my friends
> > and family, right? Fuck me for wanting to make
> > America better for the working class and for actual
> > Americans rather than oligarchs and billionaires.
> > People like you always say "like it or leave it," but
> > the option you always ignore is "Like the parts
> > worth liking, improve the parts you don't". Because
> > our country isn't perfect but that doesn't mean I'm
> > going to give up on it. You're a basic bitch bootlicker
> > and I won't be responding to your posts anymore.
> > ⊡ **Reply Share Report Save**
> > Continue this thread →

jennifersomebody ⊠ 651 points · 10 months ago
My uncle works at Citizen One and they sent out a company-
wide mNeuron message this morning saying anybody found
protesting in response to this will be terminated immediately.
That's INSANE. The protests haven't even been planned yet and
they're already squashing dissent. Hell we don't even know what

we're really protesting against really. They must have something to hide.

◱ **Reply Share Report Save**

> **chekhovswd40** ⊠ 242 points · 10 months ago
> Forgive me for being so blunt, but why does your uncle even work for them? They're f***ing evil. Hell, Ash killed their CEO. Of course they have something to hide.
> ◱ **Reply Share Report Save**

>> **jennifersomebody** ⊠ 92 points · 10 months ago
>> My dad was childhood friends with Mann. This whole thing has their whole shit fucked up. I never liked Mann, even when I was younger. I know that my dad and my uncle work for the shittiest of shitty companies but there's not much I can do about it. I'm only 17 and still live at home. :/
>> ◱ **Reply Share Report Save**

>>> **theonly420lander** ⊠ -4 points · 10 months ago
>>> "We" lol fucking wasp rich bitch out here on the ETR subreddit GTFOH. Youre part of the problem just kill yourself now
>>> ◱ **Reply Share Report Save**

>>>> **jennifersomebody** ⊠ 33 points · 10 months ago
>>>> I'm black . . . o.o
>>>> ◱ **Reply Share Report Save**

> **madeofspades99620** ⊠ 253 points · 10 months ago
> Somehow find this hard to believe . . . Your "uncle", who works at Citizen One, shared his mNeuron messages with

his 17 y/o niece? Sure . . . this has "my uncle works at Nintendo" written all over it.

⊡ **Reply Share Report Save**

> **jennifersomebody** ⊠ 40 points • 10 months ago
> Believe me or don't. Whats it matter to me? We were having breakfast and he read out the message and laughed, like, "Did they mean to send this to me?" What would I have to gain from lying about that?
>
> ⊡ **Reply Share Report Save**

> > **madeofspades99620** ⊠ 9 points • 10 months ago
> > You really think someone would do that, just on on the internet and tell lies?
> > (hint: the answer is always yes) ;)
> >
> > ⊡ **Reply Share Report Save**

6eyedbeholder ⊠ 29 points • 10 months ago
What's mneuron? Sorry if this is common knowledge i'm still in HS

⊡ **Reply Share Report Save**

> **madeofspades99620** ⊠ 15 points • 10 months ago
> mNeuron is a heavily encrypted messaging app that companies use for sensitive information. Lots of companies use it. Messages erase after a set amount of time and it's baked into the app that everything said within it is under an NDA. Her "uncle", if he's real, could get fired for telling her what was in the message.
>
> ⊡ **Reply Share Report Save**

pinkglossyvoid ⊗ 31 points · 10 months ago
Is that legal?
⊡ **Reply Share Report Save**

> **jennifersomebody** ⊗ 12 points · 10 months ago
> New York is an "employment-at-will" state, which
> means a job can fire you for basically any reason
> that isn't discrimination of a protected class. There
> might be more protections that I'm not aware
> of but the gist is, even if the reason they actually
> have for firing you is illegal, they'll just make
> something up on the official paperwork. Not sure
> if retaliating against protestors is illegal but since
> CO sent the message in mNeuron the message
> gets deleted and screenshotting is prohibited.
> ⊡ **Reply Share Report Save**

> > **pinkglossyvoid** ⊗ 4 points · 10 months ago
> > Thanks! I don't live in the US so I don't know the
> > ins and outs of your legal system. That sounds
> > BANANANAS batshit though. Crazy how much
> > power corporations have in the US.
> > ⊡ **Reply Share Report Save**

yeetnottweet ⊗ 300 points · 10 months ago
I was initially super into the idea of Ash's videos but there's been
too much collateral damage. That poor girl that got doxxed and
swatted, and now these three streamers who are probably getting
framed for her murders as we speak? She needs to donate some
of that money she stole to the normal, working class people who
have been hurt by her actions or she's dead to me.
⊡ **Reply Share Report Save**

beatthebourgeoisie ⊗ 246 points · 10 months ago

THIS THIS THIS. The key phrase here is right now. Not "until next time". Not tomorrow, not the next day. NOW. WE NEED TO DO SOMETHING NOW. IF WE GIVE UP NOW, THERE WON'T BE A NEXT TIME. IT'S RIGHT NOW. RIGHT NOW. GET INTO THE STREETS AND FUCK SOME SHIT UP. RIGHT NOW.

🖭 **Reply Share Report Save**

(Show More Comments)

[instagram.com]

⊠

isabelbellebella ✓ · Follow   . . .

isabelbellebella Protesting @ the Salisbury City Police dept in MD with what's gotta be HUNDREDS of people chanting #FreetheHunters3. Wrex and Lyss have already been released, still waiting on news about Peeps. Chant has since changed to #FreePeterKeeps.
We will not stop, we will not leave, until
ALL the hunters are free! #FreetheHunters3
#AshEatstheRich #FreePeterKeeps

43w

lyssstreamsall thank you all so much for the support!
Going home to shower and eat and then I'm coming straight back! #FREEPETERKEEPS

43w   27 likes Reply

evedabugio are those gold baseball caps . . . ETR merch?
that can't real, can it? they're monetizing Ash now?
we've come full circle . . .

43w   18 likes Reply

dosgamergummies i don't understand how they're even keeping him. Ash admitted to the murders. And if Peeps did kill them, why would he lead the police to their bodies and livestream it? Anyone with an ounce of logic sees through this immediately.

43w   15 likes   Reply
_____   Hide Replies

dootdittydootdoo @dosgamergummies Peeps livestreams like 10 hours every day.
He wouldn't have time to kill these mills and keep it from his viewers. Utter BS is what it is.

43w   5 likes   Reply

jamiedelgado @dosgamergummies
If they charge him for the murders they take the power away from Ash. Their scheme is transparent as glass and we WILLNOT FALL FOR IT.

43w   4 likes   Reply

theleftcantmemepc even if peter keeps didn't murder those businessmen, by protesting you're supporting ash and thus supporting cannibalism and murder. Disgusting.
y'all need jesus.

43w   14 likes Reply

isabelbellebella @theleftcantmemepc
How does that make any sense? We're protesting the unlawful detainment of an innocent man . . . this has nothing to do with ash.

43w   2 likes   Reply

theleftcantmemepc you're wearing gold #AshEatstheRich baseball caps. Probably made in china by slave labor or childrenor both. Keep your story straight.

43w   1 like Reply

willowslim coming down from NY, should be there in 2 hours or so. Have three cases of water in the back, plan to hand them out so no one gets dehydrated. Keep my spot warm bby!

43w   12 likes   Reply

> **isabelbellebella** @willowslim
> Wow, can't believe you were able to get off work! How long's it been since we saw each other in person!? Thanks for coming out to support the hunters!
>
> 43w   3 likes   Reply
>
>> **willowslim** @isabelbellebella
>> 6 years maybe? Since graduation?
>> Remember back in college when we spent every waking moment together?
>> Time flies . . . Anyway, I didn't get off work, they told me they couldn't find anyone to cover. But I told 'em to eff off lol.
>>
>> 43w   1 like   Reply
>>
>>> **isabelbellebella** @willowslim good for you! See you soon! <3
>>> 43w   1 like   Reply

dominicmurphy can't join in person, live in nevada. but i did send y'all 10 pizzas to keep everybody fed. (sorry but i couldn't tip the driver from the app, hopefully someone can take care of him.) Stay strong!

43w   9 likes   Reply

> **isabelbellebella** @willowslim
> Thankyousomuch! I'll take care of it.
> Even in spirit you're supporting the cause!
>
> 43w   2 likes   Reply

keepeatingtherich glad to see you wearing the merch! Check out my page for links to the hat!
We also have scarves and pins and much more!
All proceeds go to my cancer treatment!

43w   1 like   Reply

8,669 views
43w

[twitter.com]

Trending · #PeterKeeps · 5,799 tweets

FoxNews @retweetsfoxnews · **June 5**

Peter Keeps, 27 year old Twitch streamer, charged with the murders of David White, Harry Cadejo, and Rocco Mann. (foxnews.com)

3.2K Replies   **1.1K Retweets**   **4.3K Likes**

Steve the Veterinarian @vetsforvets60392 · **June 5**

#PeterKeeps did not kill those people. The man streams video games from home 10 hours a day and lifestreams with a gopro whenever he leaves his house. Perfect alibi.
THIS IS A COVERUP, AND AN OBVIOUS ONE AT THAT!
#FreePeterKeeps #JusticeforPeeps

---

10 Replies   **11 Retweets**   **31 Likes**

MSNBC @MSNBC · **June 5**

Peter Keeps, 27 year old Twitch streamer, charged with the murders of David White, Harry Cadejo, and Rocco Mann. (msnbc.com)

---

80 Replies   46 Retweets   505 Likes

James Smith @defnotarushnbot2020 · June 5

Justice is served! Hopefully #PeterKeeps rots in jail for life for what he's done to the successful, American businessmen that make our country great.

---

14 Replies   6 Retweets   7 Likes

Tanya Titania @bigtitytanya · June 5

subscribe to onlyfans within the next 42 minutes for a 42% discount on my dom/sub streams <3 #AshEatstheRich #PeterKeeps #FreePeterKeeps #FreetheHunters3 #DavidWhite #HarryCadejo #RoccoMann #CitizenOne #ComeCorrect #RisingSun (onlyfans.com)

Reply   Retweet   1 Like

CNN @CNN · June 5

Peter Keeps, 27 year old Twitch streamer, charged with the murders of David White, Harry Cadejo, and Rocco Mann. (cnn. com)

---

45 Replies   31 Retweets   251 Likes

Karl Barx @w00fw00fcomrade · June 5

The Mainstream Media, who until this point has ignored Ash, her videos, and her cause, JUMPING at the chance to report that Peter Keeps has been charged with Ash's murders. This is a miscarriage of justice. It's so obvious
#PeterKeeps is innocent!

2 Replies   23 Retweets   22 Likes

The WashingtonPost @washingtonpost · June 5

Peter Keeps, 27 year old Twitch streamer, charged with the murders of David White, Harry Cadejo, and Rocco Mann. (washingtonpost.com)

66 Replies   89 Retweets   399 Likes

Breitbart News @BreitbartNews · June 5

Peter Keeps, black 27 year old Twitch streamer, charged with the murders of David White, Harry Cadejo, and Rocco Mann. (breitbart.com)

210 Replies   26 Retweets   90 Likes

Episode 4

Betsy Ragham

LET'S DROP THE act. Get rid of the pretense. This was never a cooking show. This was never a YouTube channel about recipes to share at Thanksgiving dinner and the proper preparation of food. This was about kickstarting a revolution. This was about holding the billionaires and the bootlickers alike accountable. And in that vein, I have a few announcements.

There has been some collateral damage surrounding my videos, and for that I am sorry. I was fully prepared to be attacked, I was fully prepared for the attempts to doxx me, but I didn't think anyone other than me or the subjects of my videos would get hurt. There was a woman. I won't name her because just saying her name would probably increase the attacks against her. People thought that she was me. She isn't. She was doxxed, she was swatted, she was the target of a massive and surprisingly intense harassment campaign. This wasn't my fault, not directly at least. But I would like to apologize to her. I'm sorry.

I would like to say, fuck 4chan. Subhuman troll motherfuckers. There's a popular Backer campaign for the woman that was mistakenly doxxed, to ease the pain and trauma she's gone through. If you're interested, donate. I'm trying to signal boost without actively linking the thing, which is contradictory, now that I think about it. I'm not going to donate any of the money I stole from our oppressors, because I don't want authorities to seize it from her. But donate if you can. Again, I'm sorry. I should have guessed that something like this would have happened.

Similarly, Peter Keeps. I am not Peter Keeps. I am not a man. But you couldn't know that. I'm here, now, talking to you. So I'm obviously not Peter. The stream is live. This isn't a pre-recorded video. Though that can be faked. I thought of that.

What you're watching now is video of Betsy Ragham at a twenty-five-thousand-dollar-per-plate fundraiser for a famously pro-pipeline senator in South Carolina last week. You know who it is; I don't even want to say that asshole's name. Won't give him the satisfaction. It isn't doctored, it isn't fake. Betsy responded to the video the next day, chastising the staff there for leaking the video. Didn't address the fact that she was basically paying the man for legislation that would benefit her, only the fact that someone had the balls to tell the rest of us. Blaming the firefighters, not the arsonist. You understand.

The fundraiser was held on June 7th, days after Peter Keeps was taken into custody. You following me so far? There's no way that Peter Keeps murdered Betsy Ragham before he was taken into custody and recorded it and delayed the stream or anything like that. Keeps was arrested; Betsy was seen alive at the fundraiser days later and in a press release the following day. You might say these events are unrelated. You might ask me what Betsy Ragham has to do with any of this. Betsy Ragham wasn't eaten; Betsy Ragham didn't have a video made about her.

This is that video. If you could see under my desk, you would see that my leg is wrapped in gauze. If you could see under the gauze, you'd see an entrance and an exit wound in my thigh. Two nights ago, on June 10th, me and my team infiltrated Betsy's home in Virginia. You shouldn't be surprised that I accompanied them. I wouldn't ask them to do anything I wasn't comfortable doing myself. Betsy was the target even before Peter Keeps was arrested. I had a whole video planned where I was going to flay her and make pork rinds. Her being an oil magnate and all. It was chosen to fit a theme and I had bought a home fryer and everything.

Betsy usually doesn't have a security detail. I know this because I've been doing reconnaissance on her for months. I don't think there was a leak on my end. I think that Betsy knew that she was the type of person that I'd want to eat. I think she knew she deserved to be eaten and she was paranoid that she was next. She was right. Anyway. We infiltrated her house easily enough. I think she wanted us to get in. I think she wanted us to drop our guard so her security detail could take us out. So she could take credit with her dragon-hoarding-wealth friends and maybe cook me herself. So they could toast over my corpse and know that they were safe.

A lot of assumptions on my part, but I'm a storyteller at heart. I might be wrong about all of this. Painkillers make me talkative.

Fortunately, none of my team suffered any casualties. I'm the only one who was hurt. Excluding Betsy's security detail, but they don't count. I consider that a success. It's only a flesh wound; the bullet went in and out without hitting the bone or any major arteries. I'll live.

Let me take you to Betsy. It might take a minute, with my limp and all, but I don't want to make any edits. I want you to take everything in. I want this to be real.

Excuse the mess. I find it difficult to clean with the leg. I could hire someone, sure, but that might compromise the entire operation.

Ahh. Here we go. Betsy. Betsy, Betsy, Betsy. Don't struggle. Smile for the camera. The duct tape will hide your smile, sure, but smile with your eyes. No. Don't make that sound. That's an awful sound. Smile and I'll make it quick. There we go.

Betsy Ragham. CEO of MEGACORPS Industries. Look at that name for a second. Think of how most companies try to mask their evil by picking boring, vague-sounding, all-encompassing company names. Think of how on the nose "MEGACORPS" is. Like they're rubbing your face in it. Let's rub Betsy's face in it. As of last week, her net worth was nine point five billion dollars. Our first billionaire here at Eat the Rich.

She won't be the last. Our first woman, too, but that wasn't by design. It wasn't on purpose. She just deserves it. They all deserved it.

My leg is killing me. Jesus. Maybe I need another pill.

We'll briefly touch on all the awful things that oil tycoons do in general before we talk about what specifically Betsy has done to earn her place here. The way that oil companies actively work to undermine public confidence in climate science and the need for climate action even as their own studies show the risk of climate change is real. Oil spills throughout the Gulf of Mexico spilling millions of barrels of crude and devastating local economies and ecosystems for decades. Personal and business ties to Saudi Arabia, with its myriad human rights abuses, and—

Shut up. Shut up, Betsy. You had your time to talk. You had forty-eight years to talk and you wasted your voice. Nothing you've ever said or done has put out an ounce, an iota, of good into the world. So shut your fucking mouth.

The Pralko Pipeline, the four-billion-dollar, thousand-mile-long rape of sacred Native American sites and displacement of its peoples, this affront to humanity and to the environment that MEGACORPS shoved down America's throats—

God fucking *dammit*, shut your sniveling, snot-crusted, silver-tongued mouth. I swear to god, I can make this quick for you or I can make it last. I can really savor it. You understand? You got it? Good. Just give me a second, let me take another pill . . .

Fracking continues to be a tentpole of MEGACORPS' profit strategy despite the known risks, risks that have been known for years: contamination of groundwater, air pollution that contributes to climate change, earthquakes and fucking explosions—

Let me finish, just let me finish this thought, goddammit—

A fracking blowout in Backdraft, Texas, destroyed three houses and resulted in six deaths. When the survivors sought damages in court, MEGACORPS fought them tooth and nail, spending more on dragging the families through our broken legal system than it would have cost to just pay the damages—

QUIET. Quiet. I can't think. You know what? What's the point? You know what side you're on. I'm tired of justifying myself. I'm tired of doing research and citing myself to make a point when the people who support what I do already know and the people who are against me won't be persuaded. I'm not doing this for me. I'm doing this for *us*. This isn't about fame or notoriety or the killing or the eating or anything. I lied to you before. Eating the Rich is a metaphor. I'm performing the metaphor for you to shock you into action. We can't sit back and let them fuck us any longer. We can't sit back and let them use us and eat *us* and chew us up and spit us out any longer. I'm tired. I'm so tired. Keep squealing, pig. We're about to make bacon.

Nine and a half billion fucking dollars. Do you know how much money that is? Can you even comprehend it? I can't. Nine and a half billion. Let's break it down a bit.

A million dollars. Imagine you had a million dollars. I'd think that to many of you, a million dollars would be a life-changing amount, an amount you might not see in your entire lifetime. A million dollars. A million seconds is eleven and a half days. A billion seconds is thirty-two *years*. The difference is exponential. It's the steepest curve; it's literally unimaginable. The word billion makes it seem possible, achievable; it diminishes the scale. But it's not. It's not for people like you, anyway. No one person should have that amount of wealth. It's immoral, it's unconscionable, it's a crime against humanity.

People like Betsy don't want you to think of how much money she has when you read that forty percent of Americans would struggle to scrape together four hundred dollars for an unexpected bill. People like Betsy Ragham would have you believe that her wealth is totally unrelated to the fact that there are six hundred thousand homeless in America as of last year, and that fifty thousand of those are veterans. People like Betsy don't want you to point out the fact that for the last five years, MEGACORPS has paid zero dollars in taxes due to loopholes that her politician pals help keep in place.

Nine and a half *billion* dollars. You still can't imagine it. Let's try. Let's say you made two thousand dollars *an hour* and worked full time since the birth of Jesus Christ to right now, to today. Let's imagine you never paid taxes, you saved every penny, you never had any expenses. You just hoarded it like David and Harry and Rocco and Betsy. Can you guess how much money you'd have?

Betsy? Can you guess? Let's jog your memory. Does that help?

Eight and a half billion. You *still* wouldn't have as much as Betsy! She'd have a full bill on you! Why is this okay? Am I the crazy one here? Ignore the fact that I just stabbed a woman in the thigh; ignore the fact that I just licked her blood off the knife. Ignore that part. Am I the crazy one for trying to hold these fuckers accountable?

During the Nova-90 pandemic in 2019, they refused to close New York City public schools for over two months because they said a hundred and fourteen *thousand* children in the school system were homeless. That they relied on the school system for maybe their only meal of the day, a place to wash their clothes, a place to be that wasn't the street. Why can't we feed our children? It's not because we can't afford it. We can afford to subsidize Betsy's company and those of her peers but we can't close schools during an actual crisis because then children will starve to death?

Take this knife, for instance. I took it from one of Betsy's *many* libraries in her McMansion. Who needs a library in their house, nevermind *multiple* libraries? A modern day . . . what was that character from that book that had the library full of unread books? Hundreds of books with spines that had never been broken? I used to know, but my head is swimmy . . . Maybe another pill will help . . .

The knife. I was talking about the knife. Look at the hilt. You see these precious gems? The knife itself is worth eighty million dollars. It doesn't even have historical value! She *commissioned* it! How am I the crazy one here? Eighty million dollars. Money that could save lives, that could make the world a better place, sitting in a glass case to be forgotten, to never be used.

Well, now it's been used. I wanted to give the knife value, and Betsy's helped in that regard. Where was I? Where am I? Oh.

Fuck this. I've gotten back to spouting statistics and grandstanding. You came here for a reason; let's get to it.

Come here, Betsy. It's okay. Shh. Shh. It's okay. That's good. Just a quick slice . . . That's good. Shh. It'll all be over soon. That's good. Go to sleep. Let me get a little taste. Ash is thirsty. Eating the rich is thirsty work. Mm. Tastes good. Tastes bad, actually, but . . . metaphorically . . . it . . . I lost the thread. Fuck. I'm going to throw up.

I'm back. Now. I could've cleaned up, but I didn't. The red really matches my hair, doesn't it? I'll give you a nice thumbnail to go viral with. In the past, I've appealed to the generosity of strangers to help their fellow Americans in need. And you did a lot of good. I want to thank each and every Backer benefactor for reaching out and helping someone that's been fucked by the American healthcare system. Some of that was me distributing Rocco Mann's money back into the system, but most of it wasn't. Most of it was the kindness of strangers, and it put a smile on my face seeing so many kind people out there.

But it wasn't the right approach. I think more good could be done with the stick and not the carrot. So it's time for extortion. Listen up. If your net worth is over ten million dollars, donate one percent of your net worth to a worthy charity and you won't be next. You'll be spared. And don't pick your own slush fund charity that goes back into your own pockets. Pick one from the list that I'm posting in the description. I don't care what your yearly salary is; I don't care if you're not technically a millionaire because you have six houses but nothing liquid. I care about your net worth. One percent. It won't make a difference to you, but it'll save your life. It'll save all of our lives.

Stay hungry, friends. The time is now. Keep your eyes open. I suspect this stream will get me banned from YouTube, but things have a way of showing up where you least expect them. There's always LiveLeak.

[reddit.com]

▲ **5,840** ▼
r/videos · Posted by u/assorgrassyknoll ⊗ 9 months ago
616 comments share save hide report [removed by moderators]

EAT THE RICH EPISODE 4 - Betsy Ragham
youtube.com/watch? . . .↗

SORT BY **BEST** ▼

sharelockbones ⊗ 1,429 points · 9 months ago
CONTENT WARNING: THIS IS A FOR REAL SNUFF
FILM. The youtube link is down (understandably) but for anyone
looking for links in the comments, you've been warned. It's
INSANE that OP didn't put a content warning on this. This is on
the level of those ISIS beheading videos and people have a right to
know what they're clicking on.
🗗 **Reply Share Report Save**

> **TKOboomer09** ⊗ 972 points · 9 months ago
> Hijacking the top comment to post the **liveleak link**.
> But yeah, content warning. Ash was right that this video
> would get her banned from youtube, it was smart of her
> to livestream it rather than posting a video.
> 🗗 **Reply Share Report Save**

> > **unbannable6152** ⊗ 229 points · 9 months ago
> > Is there a reason she was smart for livestreaming it
> > vs. posting a pre-recorded video? Forgive me if I'm

being stupid here, but she was going to be banned either way.

⊡ **Reply Share Report Save**

> **grannytax45000003** ⊠ 80 points · 9 months ago
> If I had to guess, if she uploaded the video instead of livestreaming it, there's a chance that during the encoding process or whatever it would've gotten taken down before people could see it. IANAE but I assume their content filter can screen for violence or certain keywords or whatever.
> Livestreaming it ensured that the video got out there, and also shows what she says in the video, that this happened today and not before Keeps got arrested.
>
> ⊡ **Reply Share Report Save**

> > **unbannable6152** ⊠ 22 points · 9 months ago
> > IANAE?
> >
> > ⊡ **Reply Share Report Save**

> > > **grannytax45000003** ⊠ 7 points · 9 months ago
> > > I am not an engineer. I guess using acronyms doesn't really save time if you have to explain it, my bad.
> > >
> > > ⊡ **Reply Share Report Save**

rotdogjohnson ⊠ 582 points · 9 months ago
This is wild. This is going to turn so many people against her. The media now has everything they need to demonize her. Murdering a woman and drinking her blood on a livestream? That "thumbnail" she mentioned will be the

screenshot every news station uses to call her mentally deranged and undercut her message.

⊡ **Reply Share Report Save**

> **jesuisgayyy** ⊠ 304 points • 9 months ago
> I mean . . . this is what she's been doing all along. Before Betsy, she murdered and ate three people. She cooked and ate an old dude's balls. Is this the thing that's going to change someone's opinion of her? Sure, it's graphic, but all along it was: Are you okay with Ash murdering these people, or aren't you? That hasn't changed.
>
> ⊡ **Reply Share Report Save**
>
>> **rotdogjohnson** ⊠ 118 points • 9 months ago
>> If you can't tell the difference between Ash posting a faux-cooking show video where she eats tacos (even if she admits they're made from the tongue of a televangelist) and livestreaming herself slitting the throat of an elderly woman and drinking her blood, all while popping painkillers . . . I don't know what to tell you.
>>
>> ⊡ **Reply Share Report Save**
>>
>>> **jesuisgayyy** ⊠ 95 points • 9 months ago
>>> You don't have to be condescending about it. Listen, I get there's a difference. What I'm saying is I don't think it's going to change anyone's mind about what Ash and her mission is. You're either for her or you aren't. And I am. Admittedly in this video she's going HAM but maybe that's what we need right now.
>>>
>>> ⊡ **Reply Share Report Save**

rotdogjohnson ⊠ 33 points • 9 months ago

I'm not saying it's going to change pro-Ash peoples' minds. What I'm saying is, this video that's supposed to exonerate Keeps is going to be the first exposure to Ash that a lot of people have.

This is the first, undeniable proof that what Ash is doing is real, and the first thing that the news is going to report is her blood-stained shit-eating grin. It hurts her cause. That's all I'm saying.

⊟ **Reply Share Report Save**

sovereigncitizen1040 ⊠ 72 points • 9 months ago

That's because it's fake. No one's buying this serial killer story. All these lizard people are taking their ill-gotten money and faking their deaths and avoiding taxes. They're on some island in a country with no extradition and they're living it up.

⊟ **Reply Share Report Save**

mommyarmsrbrokn ⊠ 31 points • 9 months ago

Did i click on a r/conspiracy thread by mistake? How can anyone look at the Ash situation and think it's fake? The kinds of people Ash is targeting, they don't need to fake their deaths to avoid taxes. The ones who are still alive are doing it as we speak, have been doing it their entire lives. If they fake their deaths, they can't make *more* money, which is their entire reason for living. Do you think David White would be content living on an island somewhere in isolation? No, he lived

for his sermons, he fed on attention and adora-
tion and people idolizing him. There's no way
this whole thing is fake. Did you even watch the
video? Did you think that was fake?
⊡ **Reply Share Report Save**

> **sovereigncitizen1040** ⊠ 8 points · 9 months
> ago
> It's called VFX, numbnuts. Did you watch
> Jurassic Park and think "oh man, there's dino-
> saurs now?" If the lizard people are backing
> her, she has access to their money, and can hire
> a VFX team to make her videos. Your such a
> sheep it's scary.
> ⊡ **Reply Share Report Save**

> **mommyarmsrbrokn** ⊠ 24 points · 9 months
> ago
> Oh, you're one of those people. I thought you
> were using lizard people in your first post ironi-
> cally, but looking through your post history it
> seems you weren't. I'm disengaging now. Have
> a nice day.
> ⊡ **Reply Share Report Save**

> **sovereigncitizen1040** ⊠ 1 point · 9 months
> ago
> Can't handle a real debate so you pussy out.
> Typical white knight bullshit. Eat a dick.
> ⊡ **Reply Share Report Save**

NOVA-90_diet ⊠ 630 points · 9 months ago
Ash's video on Rocco was so anti-painkiller, and now she's
popping them like candy? What a hypocrite.

⊡ **Reply Share Report Save**

riprumham007 ⊠ 441 points • 9 months ago
It wasn't anti-painkiller, it was against a healthcare system
that unnecessarily gets people hooked on opioids when
they don't need them / when there are better alternatives
available. If that was your takeaway from the video then
you're flatout wrong. You're a bootlicker if you think the
way through this is to blame addicts when it's the system
that creates addicts that is at fault.
⊡ **Reply Share Report Save**

profpoofpuffpass⊠ 404 points • 9 months ago
Is bootlicker the new boomer?
⊡ **Reply Share Report Save**

katamarisensai ⊠ 450 points • 9 months ago
ok bootlicker
⊡ **Reply Share Report Save**

profpoofpuffpass⊠ 140 points • 9 months
ago
Is this a thing? Can we make this a thing?
⊡ **Reply Share Report Save**

judgebreadd ⊠ 211 points • 9 months ago
How long until Peeps is free? They can't have a case against him
after this, right?
⊡ **Reply Share Report Save**

buckfoifeast ⊠ 99 points • 9 months ago
They didn't have a case on him before. It was always a
sham. It just depends on how committed the rich are
to convincing everyone Ash doesn't exist and how many

people get into the streets to protest. Peeps isn't free, not yet.

🖰 **Reply Share Report Save**

freeguysfivefries ⊠ 152 points · 9 months ago
This is too much. I'm not a bootlicker by any stretch, I'm actually a democratic socialist, but I can't get behind this. Ash is no better than Jeffrey Dahmer, Ted Bundy, Charles Manson. She's a serial killer and the sooner she's caught the better.

🖰 **Reply Share Report Save**

> **gggggggggggggggggggggggunit** ⊠ 42 points · 9 months ago
> Hey, at least there's a female serial killer now. Ash is a champion of women's rights.
>
> 🖰 **Reply Share Report Save**

>> **alexahirsch** ⊠ 11 points · 9 months ago
>> Hey now, there's plenty of female serial killers. Carol Bundy (no relation), Velma Barfield, and Clementine Barnabet come to mind.
>>
>> 🖰 **Reply Share Report Save**

>>> **gggggggggggggggggggggggunit** ⊠ 19 points · 9 months ago
>>> Did they "come to mind", or were they the first results when you googled "female serial killers"? I've never heard of any of them, and everyone's heard of the ones posted in the original comment. My point stands.
>>>
>>> 🖰 **Reply Share Report Save**

bureauofredacted ⊠ 51 points · 9 months ago

LET'S GOOOOOO EAT THE RICH BAYBEE LAWSON
RICH WATCH YOUR BACK
⊡ **Reply Share Report Save**

[twitter.com]

Trending · Peeps · 10,722 tweets

CNN @CNN · June 16

Charges have been dropped against Peter Keeps, Twitch
streamer, after video of the murder of Betsy Ragham, CEO of
MEGACORPS, is uploaded to YouTube. (cnn.com)

119 Replies   **65 Retweets**   **992 Likes**

Peter Keeps @peepsstreams · June 16

Home and resting. I want to thank everybody for your support.
This has been wild and surreal and truthfully, pretty terrible.
Know that I do not blame Ash. Streams should resume within the
next week. Subscribe and follow for news on when that will be.

201 Replies   **708 Retweets**   **80K Likes**

Meagan Molly Hart @lotsofmeagan · June 16

Always knew that @peepsstreams was innocent!
Hope they find that ash whoever and throw her behind bars for
the hell she put Peeps through!

3 Replies   **6 Retweets**   **15 Likes**

DONATE TO DSA @nottabootlicker · June 16

Ash put HERSELF on the line and suffered a BULLET WOUND just to exonerate Peeps! And in the process took another BILLIONAIRE LEECH out of the equation!
EAT THE RICH ASH, WE STAN HARDER THAN EVER!

1 Reply   **3 Retweets**   **3 Likes**

FoxNews @retweetsfoxnews · June 16

Liberal Socialist "Ash Whatever" behind the killing of noted philanthropist Betsy Ragham, according to YouTube snuff film, exonerating Twitch streamer Peter Keeps (foxnews.com)

3.8 K Replies   **2.3K Retweets**   **4.2K Likes**

Bootstrap Security @Bootstrapsecurity · June 16

Protect yourself and your assets with bootstrap security!
Sign up for our PREMIUM PLATINUM Security Package today!

Promoted by Bootstrap Security

Jill Stein @defnotarushnbot2024 · June 16

There is no evidence that Peter Keeps and Ash Whatever

weren't working together throw them both in jail for attacking AMERICA's business moguls and promoting socialist values!!

Reply   **Retweet**   **Like**

Killian Ptolomny @killianptolomny · **June 16**

Glad that Peter Keeps was exonerated, but sickened to see all the people championing Ash Whatever. Ash slit a woman's throat open on a livestream and drank her blood— and you're cheering her on?
What has America become?

---

15 Replies   **4 Retweets**   **33 Likes**

Breitbart News @BreitbartNews · **June 16**

Peter Keeps, black 27 year old Twitch streamer, exonerated under dubious circumstances after Ash Whatever, socialist feminist YouTuber, murders an innocent oil magnate in livestream (breitbart.com)

---

195 Replies   **41 Retweets**   **162 Likes**

Karl Barx @w00fw00fcomrade · **June 16**

Good on Ash for working to #FreePeterKeeps.
Any bets on the next billionaire to hit the dust?

Is it too much to hope Lawson Rich is next on the list?

3 Replies   **14 Retweets**   **37 Likes**

[facebook.com]

Landlords for Landlords

+Join Group · · · More   Join this
group to post and comment

Recent Activity

Gary Miller
June 17, 2022

What's everyone's thoughts on this Ash Whatever situation?
My net worth is *technically* higher than ten million dollars, but
if you looked in my actual bank account you would never believe
it. I am by no means "rich". Do other landlords here believe the
threat from her is really credible?
There's no way I can afford to donate 100K to charity . . .

———————————————————————

9 Comments   3 Shares

———————————————————————

Like   Comment   Share

———————————————————————

View 7 more comments

> **Carol Golden** I also can't afford to donate 100K.
> My plan is to raise the rent on my tenants by 18%, and
> then donate the difference to a local food bank. Most of
> my tenants frequent the food bank anyway, so it's like
> their money's going right back into their pockets.
> June 17, 2022

Reginald Larson No need to actually donate the money, just post a doctored donation receipt to your social media. That's what I did. There's no way to check.
June 17, 2022

Jennifer Bresley
June 16, 2022

Seeing a lot of my friends worried about Ash Whatever's threat, so I figured I'd post here. No need to worry. The last person she killed was worth 9.5 BILLION dollars, there's no way she's going to go after small fries like us.
No one I know is really "rich", despite what their "net worth" says (what a useless number), and her whole thing is to "eat the rich". We're fine. You're fine.
Don't panic.

---

5 Comments   2 Shares

Like   Comment   Share

View 3 more comments

Carol Golden I don't know, I'm not taking the chance . . . I've decided to raise the rent on my properties and donate to the local food banks . . . just need to do the math and figure how much.better safe than sorry, and she did say "it doesn't matter how much liquid cash you have, just net worth" . . ..
June 16, 2022

Larry Pagliacci But what if it's not just her?
She has at least a special ops team, what if it's a whole
operation? Or she's backed by the goverment? I'm freaking
out here, I own thirteen properties and I *technically*
have the cash to donate 100K to charity but that will
significantly drain my coffers . . . I don't know what to
do . . .
June 16, 2022

Carol Golden
May 15, 2022

One of my tenants plays video games on the internet for a living.
I don't understand it, but he pays his bills on time for the most
part so it doesn't bother me. Problem is, last week a SWAT team
came and used a doorbuster on the door. Now, he wasn't arrested,
and it doesn't seem like he was actually doing anything illegal.
It's this thing called "swatting" where people call SWAT teams on
people as a sort of prank?
Well, you won't believe this, but he actually asked me to fix the
door. It wasn't my fault SWAT came, it was one of the people he
plays video games for on the internet. Do I have legal standing to
ask HIM to fix the door or risk invalidating his lease? There's no
way I'm paying for the door and doorframe, as it wasn't my fault
the SWAT team came in the first place.

---

8 Comments   2 Shares

Like   Comment   Share

View 6 more comments

> **Gary Whitlock** Could you call the police department and ask if they can pay to fix it? They're the ones who broke it. It doesn't seem like you or your tenant are really at fault here, but if ANYONE deserves the blame, it's your tenant and not you. It seems like the "swatting" was a result of his "job", and not your fault as the landlord.
> May 15, 2022

> **Laura Monoghan** There's no way your responsible for fixing the door. Also, his excuse seems kind of fishy. Calling a SWAT team as a "prank"? I've never heard of that. He's probably doing something illegal and they just weren't able to prove it. If you have wording about criminal activity in your property invalidating the lease, I'd look into starting the eviction process.
> May 15, 2022

Walter Wright
April 20, 2022

How much do you all throttle the heat in your apts?
It's hitting -20F in Chicago nightly here (pretty insane for april, so much for global warming) and my heating bills are astronomical compared to what they usually are. I've only been running the heat from 5PM to 9AM (when everyone is home from work) and some of my tenants have been complaining. Thing is, I was thinking of limiting the hours even more, from 9PM to 6AM (when everyone is sleeping) to offset the costs, because otherwise, I don't have the funds to do basic repairs that my tenants ALSO need.
Am I in the wrong here?

11 Comments   4 Shares

Like   Comment   Share

View 9 more comments

Charlene Kirk It's your building, you can do what
you want with it. Is there anything in the leases that
specifically says you can't throttle the heat? If not, you're
in the clear. People can wear layers when they get home
from work and then their apts will be warm when they
sleep. Sounds good enough to me.
April 20, 2022

Kitt Momney The only problem I see is the tenants that
maybe have kids? Adults can tough it out, considering
the circumstances, but kids might get sick without a
reasonable amount of heat . . . Do what feels right to you,
but keep that in consideration.
April 20, 2022

[twitter.com]

Union for the Homeless @homelessunionnyc

We have received an INFLUX of donations for homeless shelters across NYC over the last few days—donations that help ensure our shelters stay open and that food & shelter are continuing to be provided for the needy. Thank you!

1:45PM • June 20, 2022

---

16 Replies   20 Retweets   80 Likes

AK 1776 @redhatakimbo • June 20
Replying to @homelessunionnyc

BLOOD MONEY!! THAT'S BLOOD MONEY!
LITERALLY TAKING THE BLOOD OF MURDERED MEN
AND WOMEN AND FEEDING IT TO THE WELFARE
QUEENS! SHAME ON YOU!

---

6 Replies   1 Retweet   2 Likes

Hire Queer Creators! • Diane @dianesanimeavi •
June 20
Replying to @homelessunionnyc

Thank you for all the good that you do! I had to stay in a shelter for a few weeks after I came out and my parents kicked me out of

their house. I would have never survived without one. Mine is one
story among many. You're making a difference!

3 Replies   11 Retweets   8 Likes

Disgusting. Truly Disgusting @picklezandbizkits · June 20
Replying to @homelessunionnyc

Can you see who donated the money, or is it all anonymous
donations? I'd be curious to see if any of the donations were bc of
Ash's recent video . . .

2 Replies   4 Retweets   7 Likes

Ivan Tailor @sleepcomestwice · June 20
Replying to @homelessunionnyc
And @picklezandbizkits

I'd bet it's a significant percentage. Normally, rich and middle
class people alike prefer to ignore that homelessness exists at all.
Ash has done us a service, and it only took a public execution and
the threat of more to come to do it.

Reply   Retweet   1 Like

Becky Makes Movies @beckymakesmovies · June 20
Replying to @homelessunionnyc,
@picklezandbizkits, and 1 more

But it was kind of extortion, right? Can the shelters legally keep that money? It was given because of a murder threat, not out of any sort of philanthropic ideal.

Reply   **Retweet**   **Like**

Tyler Durden @fcroxmys0x • June 20
Replying to @homelessunionnyc

Burn all the homeless shelters to the ground . . . These people are leeches, bleeding all of the productive members of society dry. We'd be better of without them.

---

2 Replies   **Retweet**   **Like**

[twitch.tv]

STREAM CHAT

3:15:12 **laughterhous355**: this is a joke, right?

3:15:18 **soupersayin0342**: it has to be

3:15:25 **ghostgothgin**: idk dudes if this is a joke it's pretty fucked

3:15:28 **kayfabekevin241_542**: the gun looks pretty real

3:15:34 **soupersayin0342**: james owns a gun, he's talked about it before

3:15:40 **soupersayin0342**: no idea if the one on stream is the one he's talked about before tho

3:15:50 **laughterhous355**: has he ever streamed this late? what time is it in america rn

3:15:53 **kayfabekevin241_542**: it's 3 in the morning

3:15:59 **kayfabekevin241_542**: i'm only here because i'm pulling an all nighter for a test

3:16:05 **kayfabekevin241_542**: i saw the stream go live and i wanted to see what was up

3:16:20 **chicogringodingo**: yeah i live in france and i never get to see james stream live

3:16:26 **chicogringodingo**: always watch the VODs so was surprised to see him streaming

3:16:33 **SUPRIIOTSUPRHOT**: just got here, what's going on

3:16:37 **laughterhous355**: fuck if we know dude

3:16:41 **ghostgothgin**: im freaking out guys is he fr?

3:16:45 **dubstebdarryl054**: james went live like ten mins ago

3:16:49 **dubstebdarryl054**: said that his landlord is evicting him

3:16:51 **vapetrixrfrkidz**: that gun is 100% real

3:16:53 **dubstebdarryl054**: bc he refused to pay for the door the police broke when he was swatted last time

3:16:56 **vapetrixrfrkidz**: it's a glock 17

3:17:00 **dubstebdarryl054**: started ranting saying that ash has the right idea

3:17:04 **soupersayin0342**: he's mentioned having a glock before so checks out

3:17:08 **dubstebdarryl054**: literally said "eat the rich, we gotta eat the rich" for like five mins straight

3:17:09 **soupersayin0342**: that means this prolly isn't a joke

3:17:11 **ghostgothgin**: so are any of us gonna call the police?

3:17:16 **vapetrixrfrkidz**: he could probably sell that gun and fix the door himself

3:17:20 **dubstebdarryl054**: the rest of the time he was setting up the gopro headset

3:17:22 **vapetrixrfrkidz**: or sell any part of his streaming setup to just get a new fking door

3:17:28 **dubstebdarryl054**: unlocking his gun safe and loading the gun

3:17:30 **SUPRHOTSUPRHOT**: this is fucking nuts

3:17:32 **kayfabekevin241_542**: i'm out guys not looking to watch someone get fr murdered

3:17:34 **SUPRHOTSUPRHOT**: surreal

3:17:36 **alwaysbluealwaysblue**: i've always said that this is the problem with ash

3:17:39 **chicogringodingo**: me too guys, shits getting too real for me

3:17:42 **alwaysbluealwaysblue**: she was always going to inspire copycat killings

3:17:50 **ghostgothgin**: anyone know james last name? im calling the police

3:17:58 **SUPRHOTSUPRHOT**: narc

3:18:01 **dubstebdarryl054**: snitches get stiches

3:18:02 **vapetrixrfrkidz**: lmao bootlicker bitch get fucked

3:18:06 **alwaysbluealwaysblue**: this isn't like betsy ragham, this is just some rando landlord

3:18:10 **vapetrixrfrkidz**: all landlords are bad

3:18:13 **SUPRHOTSUPRHOT**: ALAB

3:18:18 **dubstebdarryl054**: landlords contribute nothing to society

3:18:21 **dubstebdarryl054**: all they do is own land and bleed the working class

3:18:25 **alwaysbluealwaysblue**: it's just a job dude, like any other job

3:18:30 **alwaysbluealwaysblue**: someone has to do it

3:18:34 **soupersayin0342**: what do y'all have against landlords

3:18:37 **vapetrixrfrkidz**: GET FUUUUUUUUCKED

3:18:42 **laughterhous355**: well, there he goes

3:18:46 **laughterhous355**: guess we're going to find out one way or the other

3:18:48 **soupersayin0342**: sounds like y'all a bunch of salty jobless dicks

3:18:49 **vapetrixrfrkidz**: LET'S GOOOO

3:18:50 **ghostgothgin**: wtf

3:18:55 **ghostgothgin**: 911 hung up on me, said that prank calling emergency services is a crime

3:18:57 **ghostgothgin**: WTF

3:18:59 **SUPRHOTSUPRHOT**: i'm a homeowner motherfucker i just rented an apt for years and know how shitty landlords are

3:19:05 **dubstebdarryl054**: james has been swatted like 4 times so maybe they thought you were joking?

3:19:06 **rancorrampage37643**: what game is this?

3:19:09 **vapetrixrfrkidz**: EAT THE RICH EAT THE RICH

3:19:12 **ghostgothgin**: thats fucking stupid

3:19:16 **laughterhous355**: how is this stream still up? are twitch mods just not awake right now?

3:19:20 **bradbeforetime**: this is some french revolution shit

3:19:22 **rancorrampage37643**: what game is this?

3:19:25 **vapetrixrfrkidz**: EAT THE RICH EAT THE RICH

3:19:28 **soupersayin0342**: ill try calling the cops too

3:19:31 **alwaysbluealwaysblue**: except that was against kings and this is against some rando landlord, do you hear yourself brad?

3:19:33 **vapetrixrfrkidz**: HELL YEAH BRAD BRING OUT THE GUILLOTINE

3:19:36 **SUPRHOTSUPRHOT**: where'd he get a key for her door?

3:19:40 **ghostgothgin**: oh wow he's really doing it

3:19:42 **ghostgothgin**: i can't watch

3:19:43 **SUPRHOTSUPRHOT**: should've broken it down with a doorbuster

3:19:44 **vapetrixrfrkidz**: EAT THE RICH EAT THE RICH

3:19:45 **rancorrampage37643**: what game is this?

3:19:47 **SUPRHOTSUPRHOT**: make it real poetic and shit

3:19:50 **laughterhous355**: IT'S NOT A GAME RANCOR

3:19:52 **dubstebdarryl054**: rancor its not a game its a gopro

3:19:55 **alwaysbluealwaysblue**: james is about to catch a case on some bullshit

3:19:57 **dubstebdarryl054**: james said he was gonna murder his landlord

3:19:58 **alwaysbluealwaysblue**: OVER A DOOR

3:20:20 **vapetrixrfrkidz**: EAT THE RICH EAT THE RICH

3:20:22 **sn4fub4r00**: aaaand she's awake

3:20:24 **rancorrampage37643**: what game is this?

3:20:26 **ghostgothgin**: jesus christ

3:20:26 **soupersayin0342**: cops are on their way

3:20:28 **vapetrixrfrkidz**: LET'S GOOOOOOO

3:20:32 **dubstebdarryl054**: fuck fuck fuck

3:20:34 **ghostgothgin**: he really fucking killed her

3:20:36 **laughterhous355**: this can't be real

3:20:39 **vapetrixrfrkidz**: THE REVOLUTION'S STARTING BAYBEEE

3:20:40 **rancorrampage37643**: what game is this?

3:20:41 **ghostgothgin**: jesus christ

3:20:41 **laughterhous355**: this CAN'T be real

3:20:42 **vapetrixrfrkidz**: EAT THE RICH EAT THE RICH
EAT THE RICH

[newsbyconews.com]

Foodrunner driver, 25, jailed after latest in surge of copycat killings
By Wally Striker | NEWSBYCO
Updated 2:43 PM ET, Mon July 4, 2022

(NEWSBYCO) — Jennifer Cortez, driver for the food delivery app Foodrunner, was jailed and charged with the murder of Sophia Peterson, marketing consultant for Foodrunner on Sunday, according to local police. This is the sixth and latest in a string of copycat killings inspired by serial killer "Ash Whatever" in her "Eat the Rich" series on YouTube.

Cortez, an artist that sells her art online through sites like Shopify and Etsy, was contacted by Peterson two months ago after seeing her portfolio on her website. According to Cortez, she was contracted to redesign some of the marketing materials for Foodrunner and was promised a flat fee of $2000, but after completing the assets was told that "the exposure" of being associated with Foodrunner was payment enough . . ..
Read more . . .

You need a subscription to continue reading this article.

Covering the news and helping citizens stay informed costs money. For journalists, for staff, for server costs, etc. Please support NEWSBYCO in order to stay informed.

Keep reading for ~~$50~~ $5

Cancel any time. Seriously. If at any time you don't feel informed, or don't support our mission, you can cancel your support (as dictated by US law).

More Offers | Already a subscriber? **Sign in.**

Sponsored Stories You may like   Ad Content by Barabos

— 13 Badass Women That FIRED BACK Against The Patriarchy!

— 16 Ways To Survive In The Gig Economy! You Won't Believe How Much These Apps Are Paying!

— Sell Your Unused Diabetic Test Strips For $$$!

— 9 Reasons You NEED Bootstrap Security To Protect Yourself And Your Assets!

— 10 Tips For A Successful Backer Campaign That You'd Never Guess!

Get in on the Conversation! (2,302)

CharlotteCarr 4m
These millennials are all entitled snowflakes. Surely the increased income she would receive with the exposure from working with such a large company would be better than spending a life behind bars. This is getting ridiculous.
Reply • Share • Report

162

ErikwithAK 4m
ANOTHER ONE? I'm a business owner and I'm getting scared
sh*tless seeing all these stories. I own three restaurants but I am
not "rich". Sure I'm rich compared to these zoomers living in their
cars because they can't budget but people like me don't deserve to
live in fear because we're successful.
Reply • Share • Report

ROCKFLAGNEAGLE 6m
Maybe these commies should move to venezuela if they hate
capitalism so much. See what communism REALLY does to
a country.
Reply • Share • Report

butterymails454545 7m
These assholes aren't even copycat killers. The whole point of Eat
the Rich is to EAT THE RICH. This b***h just shot her. GO
ALL THE WAY IF YOURE GONNA GO NUTS WHATS THE
POINT OTHERWISE
Reply • Share • Report

CupcakeConnie79 9m
Hope they're all running scared. This has been a long
time coming.
Reply • Share • Report

OBUMMADIDNOVA90 10m
ALL THESE KIDS WANT ARE HANDOUTS,,, IN MY
DAY I WORKED A JOB DURING SUMMERS TO PAY
FOR COLLEGE AND ALL THAT HARD WORK LET ME
BUY A HOUSE WHEN I GRADUATED,,, I DIDNT GET
NO HANDOUTS
Reply • Share • Report

annabambabam 12m

I don't think this is what Ash wants . . . the people she killed were all millionaires and billionaires . . . I think a 'marketing consultant' for an app doesn't really fit that bill . . .

Reply • Share • Report

SHOW MORE COMMENTS . . .

[instagram.com]

☒

SECOURSWILDLIFE ✓ · Follow   . . .

SECOURSWILDLIFE This is Annabelle the wombat, who was displaced from her home by wildfires earlier this year. Feeding and housing wildlife displaced by wildfires isn't cheap, but thanks to your donations animals like Annabelle have new homes and full bellies!

Follow us on Facebook or donate **here.**

36w

figthefaethless92001 So cute! I'd donate if I didn't just donate to the WWF earlier this week! Will try to signal boost tho :)))

36w   9 likes   Reply
——   Hide Replies

> **babyface_____brett4** @figthefaethless92001 What does wrestling have to do with wombats?
>
> 36w   3 likes   Reply

senorameeseeks____1 This whole situation with Ash has totally changed my opinion of all my favorite charities . . . are you saving these animals with blood money? You need to tell us where the money is coming from . . . I don't want to be complicit in stochastic terrismby supporting you guys . . .

36w   1 like   Reply

victor.haynes SO CUTE. Are you allowed to own wombats as pets? I want one.

36w   1 like   Reply

blainthemonorail43023 My brother's a volunteer firefighter and has been fighting these wildfires over the last couple of years and this is why he does it . . . people don't realize it's not just about the human cost (which is important, don't get me wrong) . . . but several billion animals died in the wildfires in Australia over the last few years. This is happening year round now . . .
We need to take care of the planet and our animal brothers and sisters!

36w   9 Likes   Reply

percy_stacy.grant does anyone else remember when the phone companies were throttling data to the firefighters fighting the wildfires? Pepperidge farms remembers . . .

36w   6 Likes   Reply

>   **sufyanrivers830** @percy_stacy.grant
>   So what you're saying is . . .#eattherich?
>
>   36w   4 likes   Reply

dixonnixonandwight never knew that's what A wombat looked like! You learn something new every day!

36w   Like   Reply

4,302 views
36w

[discord.com]

#19-00004-80806002370

Justin 08/01/22
alright guys i'm off for the night

Justin 08/01/22
peace

Bobby 08/01/22
me too i gotta be up in the morning

BustinMakesMe 08/01/22
I got another match in me if anyone wants to keep going

BustinMakesMe 08/01/22
Guess not

MATT@TTACK 08/04/22
yo

Justin 08/04/22
sup dude

Bobby 08/04/22
what's goooooood jsut got off work you wanna play

MATT@TTACK 08/04/22
is brian on?

Bobby 08/04/22
says he's online but he's not answering, maybe taking a shit

MATT@TTACK 08/04/22
gotta talk to you guys about something

BustinMakesMe 08/04/22
You guessed right bobs lol

BustinMakesMe 08/04/22
Just blew my toilet the FUCK up

Justin 08/04/22
so you're finally coming out matt?

Justin 08/04/22
gotta say, it's about time

MATT@TTACK 08/04/22
nah man this is serious

Bobby 08/04/22
being true to yourself is VERY serious matt

Bobby 08/04/22
you love who you love man none of us are going to judge

MATT@TTACK 08/04/22
can you guys shut the fuck up for a second and listen

BustinMakesMe 08/04/22
Can I just say

BustinMakesMe 08/04/22
You're sounding very homophobic right now

BustinMakesMe 08/04/22
Your friends are here for you and we just want to be supportive

MATT@TTACK 08/04/22
you know what neverfuckingmind

Justin 08/04/22
sorrysorry what's up man you okay

MATT@TTACK 08/04/22
okay so i got fired this morning

BustinMakesMe 08/04/22
Shit man that sucks

Bobby 08/04/22
fuck i'm sorry dude

MATT@TTACK 08/04/22
thanks but that's not the point

Justin 08/04/22
you need a place to crash? my couch is always open

Bobby 08/04/22
why'd they fire you

MATT@TTACK 08/04/22
thanks justin but im not there yet

MATT@TTACK 08/04/22
well, they came up with some bullshit but i know its cuz i called
in sick last week

MATT@TTACK 08/04/22
its like, we work with food, i had the flu, you want me to come in

MATT@TTACK 08/04/22
and get all the people on the line sick?

MATT@TTACK 08/04/22
and then everybodys out instead of just me?

BustinMakesMe 08/04/22
Not only that but the customers too

MATT@TTACK 08/04/22
exactly

BustinMakesMe 08/04/22
They can't fire you for being sick tho

MATT@TTACK 08/04/22
well they said its cuz i was late this morning and i have a "history" with being late

MATT@TTACK 08/04/22
it was literally thirty seconds and its cuz the transit system here sucks balls

MATT@TTACK 08/04/22
but i could tell it was cuz i called out and they were just looking for any reason to can my ass

Justin 08/04/22
that can't be legal?

BustinMakesMe 08/04/22

NY is a "right-to-work" state they can fire you for literally any reason

BustinMakesMe 08/04/22
That isn't like, being part of a protected class or something

Justin 08/04/22
right right right that's super fucked

MATT@TTACK 08/04/22
so i hit up my dealer on the way back home

MATT@TTACK 08/04/22
to pick up some bud because my anxiety is fucking me

BustinMakesMe 08/04/22
As you do

Bobby 08/04/22
understandable

MATT@TTACK 08/04/22
and as he's weighing out he asks me if i'm on the dark web at all

BustinMakesMe 08/04/22
Uhoh

Bobby 08/04/22
lmaooo like onion and tor and all that shit

MATT@TTACK 08/04/22
yeah

Justin 08/04/22

whats the dark web

BustinMakesMe 08/04/22
Like, where all the shady shit goes down on the internet

BustinMakesMe 08/04/22
Technically it's the websites that aren't indexed by google and not accessible unless you know where to look

BustinMakesMe 08/04/22
But most people who use it use it to get drugs

Bobby 08/04/22
and child porn. don't forget child porn

MATT@TTACK 08/04/22
i mean, yeah. technically. that's the most reductive answer you can give but sure

MATT@TTACK 08/04/22
it's where the illegal shit goes down on the internet

MATT@TTACK 08/04/22
steve isn't a pedophile so he uses it to get drugs

Justin 08/04/22
how does that work

Justin 08/04/22
wouldn't the police just go to those same sites and bust them

MATT@TTACK 08/04/22
there's ways to mask your ip and make yourself anonymous

MATT@TTACK 08/04/22
LISTEN this isn't a TED talk i'm not here to teach you assholes
what the dark web is

Bobby 08/04/22
lol ok dude get to the point

MATT@TTACK 08/04/22
so i tell him no, i'm too paranoid and idk how to use tor or
whatever the new shit is to make sure i don't get busted

MATT@TTACK 08/04/22
i went on silk road back in the day but was too chickenshit to
actually order anything

BustinMakesMe 08/04/22
My roommate in college used to order shit on silk road before it
got shut down

BustinMakesMe 08/04/22
Shady as shiiiiit

Bobby 08/04/22
before you dropped out?

BustinMakesMe 08/04/22
Yeah before i dropped out

BustinMakesMe 08/04/22
Still chipping away at those student loans

MATT@TTACK 08/04/22
so he's weighing me out, and he starts talking about how all these
sites have like, sections where you can put out hits on people

MATT@TTACK 08/04/22
and how theyre usually just scams or ploys by police to catch
spurned spouses or whatever

Justin 08/04/22
okay . . .

MATT@TTACK 08/04/22
but that three days ago the listings BLEW UP

MATT@TTACK 08/04/22
like, hundreds, maybe thousands, of contracts all listed at the
same time

BustinMakesMe 08/04/22
Yeah you see that netflix show about the guy that scammed like
30 people by taking contracts and just dipping with the $$$

MATT@TTACK 08/04/22
all for high profile, rich af assholes

BustinMakesMe 08/04/22
It was good but maybe an episode or two too long

Justin 08/04/22
oh shit so like some eat the rich type shit? you think it was ash?

MATT@TTACK 08/04/22
maybe

MATT@TTACK 08/04/22
probably

MATT@TTACK 08/04/22
but he's showing me one of the sites and GUESS WHO TF
I SAW

Justin 08/04/22
me

Bobby 08/04/22
you

MATT@TTACK 08/04/22
javits berkeley

Justin 08/04/22
NO

BustinMakesMe 08/04/22
HAHAHAHA

Justin 08/04/22
NO WAY

BustinMakesMe 08/04/22
FUCK YOUUUU DUUUUUUDE

Bobby 08/04/22
whos javits berkeley

MATT@TTACK 08/04/22
THE ASSHOLE WHO GOT MY MOM FIRED FROM
HER JOB

Bobby 08/04/22

hahahahahaa no wayyy

Justin 08/04/22
how much for killing that fuckbag

MATT@TTACK 08/04/22
you're never gonna believe this

BustinMakesMe 08/04/22
The anticipation is killing me

MATT@TTACK 08/04/22
one million dollars

Bobby 08/04/22
ok doctor evil

BustinMakesMe 08/04/22
Lmaoooo I'd do that shit for free

MATT@TTACK 08/04/22
that's what i'm talkin about boys

MATT@TTACK 08/04/22
you know what we could do with a million dollars?

BustinMakesMe 08/04/22
Defff lemme just grab my ak

BustinMakesMe 08/04/22
Today was a good day

MATT@TTACK 08/04/22
i'm serious

Bobby 08/04/22

dude you're a vegetarian and youre talking about mercing some stock broker?

MATT@TTACK 08/04/22

animals are innocent

MATT@TTACK 08/04/22

this motherfucker isnt

BustinMakesMe 08/04/22

Wait you're serious

MATT@TTACK 08/04/22

dead serious

MATT@TTACK 08/04/22

dude my mom lost her HOUSE because of this racist mfer

MATT@TTACK 08/04/22

claimed she was stealing from him

MATT@TTACK 08/04/22

you know my mom

MATT@TTACK 08/04/22

do you think she stole this dudes watch

Justin 08/04/22

no fucking way dude your moms a saint

MATT@TTACK 08/04/22

and then he got her blacklisted from cleaning houses
ANYWHERE else

MATT@TTACK 08/04/22
my moms been cleaning houses for thirty years, since she moved
to this fucking country, and one word from this rich asshole and
she can't get a job cleaning anywhere except for like odd jobs
for randos

MATT@TTACK 08/04/22
that was my parents only source of income, my dad cant work,
you guys know that

Bobby 08/04/22
shit i knew he got her fired but not the second part

Bobby 08/04/22
that sucks dude im sorry

BustinMakesMe 08/04/22
Let me just play along for a minute

BustinMakesMe 08/04/22
And forget that what you're saying is batshit bananas

BustinMakesMe 08/04/22
Because you're sounding increasingly serious

MATT@TTACK 08/04/22
shoot bro i got this all figured out

BustinMakesMe 08/04/22
Doesnt javits live in some penthouse in the city

BustinMakesMe 08/04/22
How would we even get inside

MATT@TTACK 08/04/22
he does live in a penthouse in the city

MATT@TTACK 08/04/22
but he has a summer house upstate

MATT@TTACK 08/04/22
which is the house my mom worked at

Bobby 08/04/22
is this the beginning of a guy ritchie movie before the whole plan goes sideways and were on the run for our lives?

BustinMakesMe 08/04/22
Waitwaitwait

BustinMakesMe 08/04/22
Didn't your moms boss never get the key back from your mom

MATT@TTACK 08/04/22
yup

MATT@TTACK 08/04/22
and remember kayla made a joke about how we should actually rob him because we might as well do the thing he accused my mom of

MATT@TTACK 08/04/22
because the summer house has ZERO security, only a key and the security system, which my mom knows the code for . . .

Bobby 08/04/22
is he at the summer house now?

MATT@TTACK 08/04/22
yupyupyup

MATT@TTACK 08/04/22
i know because my moms old boss was bitching to her about
how the dude STILL complains to her about my mom and his
stupid watch

MATT@TTACK 08/04/22
calls her "that spic cunt you hired that stole from me"

BustinMakesMe 08/04/22
WoooowwWWW

MATT@TTACK 08/04/22
and my moms old boss desperately wants to stand up for my
mom but can't afford to lose her job too

Justin 08/04/22
i dont . . . dude

Justin 08/04/22
are we seriously talking about this?

Justin 08/04/22
in DISCORD of all places?

BustinMakesMe 08/04/22
So wait didn't you say before that most of these listings are fake

BustinMakesMe 08/04/22

Before we even consider this how do you know that these are legit

Justin 08/04/22
CONSIDERING?

Justin 08/04/22
WHAT ARE YOU TALKING ABOUT?

Bobby 08/04/22
do any of you even own guns? where would we even start

MATT@TTACK 08/04/22
well hold on im getting there

MATT@TTACK 08/04/22
17 of these contracts have been filled out already

MATT@TTACK 08/04/22
and as people are getting paid the news is getting around that this
is all legit

MATT@TTACK 08/04/22
and people are scrambling to claim these contracts

Justin 08/04/22
17!?!

MATT@TTACK 08/04/22
and the reason he was even telling me this in the first place

MATT@TTACK 08/04/22
yeah 17

MATT@TTACK 08/04/22

theres a site like "ashs specials menu" or something thats tracking whos been got so far

MATT@TTACK 08/04/22
ill link you later

Bobby 08/04/22
kind of on the nose but okay

MATT@TTACK 08/04/22
but the reason he was telling me in the first place

MATT@TTACK 08/04/22
is cuz HIS contact took a contract and got paid out

MATT@TTACK 08/04/22
and skipped the country

MATT@TTACK 08/04/22
so he was saying that he might be dry for a while

BustinMakesMe 08/04/22
Whoa

BustinMakesMe 08/04/22
So whenre we doing this

Justin 08/04/22
youre just gonna take his word?

Justin 08/04/22
"a friend of a friend assassinated some rich asshole and definitely got paid through the internet for it"

Justin 08/04/22
this is some "my uncle works at nintendo" bullshit

MATT@TTACK 08/04/22
not just any rich asshole

MATT@TTACK 08/04/22
pierce pattinson

BustinMakesMe 08/04/22
The senator??????????

Bobby 08/04/22
shit i saw that on the news

Bobby 08/04/22
the asshole whos invested in that company?

Bobby 08/04/22
whats it called

BustinMakesMe 08/04/22
Satellite Umbrella

BustinMakesMe 08/04/22
The company that bought out the company that invented the nova90 vaccine and then charged thousands of dollars for it

Justin 08/04/22
who knows if that was actually one of these contracts

Justin 08/04/22
maybe it was ash herself

MATT@TTACK 08/04/22
maybe

MATT@TTACK 08/04/22
all my guy knows is his guy suddenly came into 3 mil in crypto

MATT@TTACK 08/04/22
and disappeared

Bobby 08/04/22
jesus

Bobby 08/04/22
3 mil would pay off all my debt a hundred times over

Bobby 08/04/22
id finally be able to breathe

Bobby 08/04/22
maybe buy a house

MATT@TTACK 08/04/22
exactlyyyy dude

Justin 08/04/22
well that guy clearly deserved it

Justin 08/04/22
what has javits done besides just be kind of a dick to your mom

MATT@TTACK 08/04/22
kind of a dick?

MATT@TTACK 08/04/22

dude this guy ruined my moms life

MATT@TTACK 08/04/22
my mom was the embodiment of the american dream

MATT@TTACK 08/04/22
moved here with nothing, got a job and through sheer hard work
bought a house and raised a family

Bobby 08/04/22
still is bro. she still is.

MATT@TTACK 08/04/22
30 years of work

MATT@TTACK 08/04/22
destroyed overnight by this wasp motherfucker with a
single accusation

BustinMakesMe 08/04/22
Yeah I mean I knew the story before but the way you're framing it

BustinMakesMe 08/04/22
Is pissing me off

Justin 08/04/22
okayokay sorry i worded that bad

MATT@TTACK 08/04/22
And then YEARS later is still badmouthing her to her friend,
calling her a "spic cunt", lording over her that she can't defend her
friend without also losing her job

Justin 08/04/22

i'm just trying to steer you guys away from a decision youll regret

Bobby 08/04/22
yeah when you put it like that

Bobby 08/04/22
if hes being that misogynistic and racist in public, what kinda shit is he saying and doing when no ones looking

MATT@TTACK 08/04/22
exactly

MATT@TTACK 08/04/22
when people show you who they are, believe them

Justin 08/04/22
dont quote maya angelou at me

Justin 08/04/22
to justify murdering someone

Justin 08/04/22
FOH with that shit

BustinMakesMe 08/04/22
The most important thing is

BustinMakesMe 08/04/22
None of us have guns

BustinMakesMe 08/04/22
And I don't know to store/sell crypto

MATT@TTACK 08/04/22

welllll steve said he'd give us pistols

MATT@TTACK 08/04/22
dispose of them after

MATT@TTACK 08/04/22
and deal with the actual site/crypto selling/all that shit

Justin 08/04/22
for the last time guys, don't do this shit

Justin 08/04/22
would you rather be in debt or be in jail

MATT@TTACK 08/04/22
for 20%

Justin 08/04/22
this fucker isnt worth it

BustinMakesMe 08/04/22
So 200K? And then the rest of us get 200K each?

BustinMakesMe 08/04/22
SIGN

MATT@TTACK 08/04/22
justin, i don't think you understand

BustinMakesMe 08/04/22
ME

BustinMakesMe 08/04/22
UP

MATT@TTACK 08/04/22
the money is an incentive, sure

MATT@TTACK 08/04/22
but this is literally about revenge for me

MATT@TTACK 08/04/22
you know how often ive fantasized about killing this prick?

Bobby 08/04/22
i mean i think we need to have a conversation off discord

Bobby 08/04/22
in person

MATT@TTACK 08/04/22
and now someone has given me the means not only to get that fucker back

Bobby 08/04/22
but i think im in

MATT@TTACK 08/04/22
but for literally an amount of money that will change my life immeasurably for the better

Justin 08/04/22
you guys are joking right? this is just one of those hypotheticals you work your way through

Justin 08/04/22
for funsies

BustinMakesMe 08/04/22
Yeah dude 200K fixes literally every problem in my life right now

Justin 08/04/22
And im the sucker that takes the joke too seriously and then you all laugh at me

MATT@TTACK 08/04/22
this is some john wick shit

Justin 08/04/22
and then i say "oh you guys you got me"

Justin 08/04/22
BUT JOHN WICK WAS AN ASSASSIN

Bobby 08/04/22
nah dude if this is happening im all the way in

Justin 08/04/22
AND YOURE A LINE COOK

Justin 08/04/22
brians an electrician

Justin 08/04/22
and bobbys a fucking office manager

MATT@TTACK 08/04/22
like i said before

MATT@TTACK 08/04/22
i dont think you understand

Bobby 08/04/22
i mean i play a lot of cod my k/d is pretty high ngl

MATT@TTACK 08/04/22
because you don't have the same kind of debt that the rest of
us do

Bobby 08/04/22
i think i can shoot one wasp

MATT@TTACK 08/04/22
this kind of debt . . . it hangs over you

MATT@TTACK 08/04/22
its like a storm that never dissipates

MATT@TTACK 08/04/22
i think about it all day

MATT@TTACK 08/04/22
i think about it falling asleep at night

BustinMakesMe 08/04/22
It's crushing

MATT@TTACK 08/04/22
i dream about it

BustinMakesMe 08/04/22
I literally feel a weight pressing down on my chest anytime it pops
into my head

MATT@TTACK 08/04/22
its the first thing i think about when i wake up in the morning

BustinMakesMe 08/04/22
Which happens multiple times every day

Bobby 08/04/22
my paycheck every week just pays down the interest

Bobby 08/04/22
not even that

Bobby 08/04/22
i literally owe more money now than i did six years ago

MATT@TTACK 08/04/22
exactly

MATT@TTACK 08/04/22
the worst part about it is the shame

BustinMakesMe 08/04/22
I sometimes find myself crying without even realizing i started

MATT@TTACK 08/04/22
and the resignation that this is just what my life is now

Bobby 08/04/22
exactly, the shame

Bobby 08/04/22
my family keeps asking me when i'm going to buy a house

Bobby 08/04/22
and start a family

MATT@TTACK 08/04/22
and the answer you give is always "some day"

MATT@TTACK 08/04/22
but you know the real answer is "ill never be able to"

Bobby 08/04/22
they give me shit for taking out so many loans to go to school for an art degree

Bobby 08/04/22
when i have a job that doesnt have anything to do with art

Bobby 08/04/22
and im like bitch you told me i HAD to go to college

Bobby 08/04/22
and that i should follow my passion

Bobby 08/04/22
and if you love what you do youll never work a day in your life

BustinMakesMe 08/04/22
Exactly i didnt even want to go to college

BustinMakesMe 08/04/22
I went cause my parents generation said thats what you do

Bobby 08/04/22
THEY LIED TO US

BustinMakesMe 08/04/22
I went to school for communications

BustinMakesMe 08/04/22
COMMUNICATIONS

BustinMakesMe 08/04/22
I STILL DONT KNOW WHAT THAT MEANS

MATT@TTACK 08/04/22
and like

MATT@TTACK 08/04/22
i didn't ask to get in that car accident

MATT@TTACK 08/04/22
drunk driver, totally not my fault

MATT@TTACK 08/04/22
and somehow i get stuck with an 80K hospital bill because the
healthcare system in this country is FUCKED

BustinMakesMe 08/04/22
and now your life is fucked over something that wasnt in
your control

Bobby 08/04/22
and somehow WE get blamed for it

Bobby 08/04/22
millenials are killing the housing industry

Bobby 08/04/22
we're killing the diamond industry

Bobby 08/04/22
we're killing the restaurant industry

BustinMakesMe 08/04/22
If millennials didn't eat so much goddamn avocado toast and knew how to budget

BustinMakesMe 08/04/22
Theyd be able to buy houses like we were able to

BustinMakesMe 08/04/22
Bitch I ate instant ramen for dinner four times last week

BustinMakesMe 08/04/22
This aint about BUDGETING

Bobby 08/04/22
"i was able to pay my way through college and start a family and buy a house why cant you"

Bobby 08/04/22
motherfucker you got a part time job over the summer at some factory

Bobby 08/04/22
and were able to use those wages to pay for college

Bobby 08/04/22
AND make enough to get a down payment for a house by the time you graduated

Justin 08/04/22
had no idea it was so bad for you guys

BustinMakesMe 08/04/22

And my dads income was somehow enough that my mom was able to stay at home and raise us

Bobby 08/04/22
i worked three jobs through college and barely was able to afford a studio

Bobby 08/04/22
and somehow im the lazy one?

BustinMakesMe 08/04/22
Which im so thankful for im lucky in a lot of ways

BustinMakesMe 08/04/22
But that life isnt possible anymore

MATT@TTACK 08/04/22
yeah like al bundy was a shoe salesman and somehow afforded that fucking house

MATT@TTACK 08/04/22
miserable all the fucking time

MATT@TTACK 08/04/22
boomer ass grateful for nothing fuck

Justin 08/04/22
well

Justin 08/04/22
you guys are right

Justin 08/04/22
i guess i dont understand

Bobby 08/04/22
so youre in?

BustinMakesMe 08/04/22
LETS GO BAYBEEE

MATT@TTACK 08/04/22
JUSTINS IN ALRIGHT

Justin 08/04/22
no

Justin 08/04/22
I mean

Justin 08/04/22
i'm not a rat

Justin 08/04/22
as far as im concerned this conversation never happened

Bobby 08/04/22
wait what

Justin 08/04/22
but i cant be a part of it

MATT@TTACK 08/04/22
wait come on dude

BustinMakesMe 08/04/22
Shit he went offline

Bobby 08/04/22
so what does that mean for . . . this

Bobby 08/04/22
can we trust him?

MATT@TTACK 08/04/22
def

MATT@TTACK 08/04/22
weve known each other since middle school

MATT@TTACK 08/04/22
as long as we dont keep him in the loop he wont talk

Bobby 08/04/22
coolcoolcool

BustinMakesMe 08/04/22
So what is that . . . 265K each now?

Bobby 08/04/22
and change

MATT@TTACK 08/04/22
worrrrrd

BustinMakesMe 08/04/22
Okay well we need to meet in person

BustinMakesMe 08/04/22
Justin was right talking about this shit in discord was stupid

Bobby 08/04/22

when

MATT@TTACK 08/04/22
lmao im down whenever i dont have a joooob

BustinMakesMe 08/04/22
Okay

BustinMakesMe 08/04/22
Ill text you guys tomm

Bobby 08/04/22
k

MATT@TTACK 08/04/22
k

BustinMakesMe 08/04/22
Peace

Bobby 08/04/22
ttyl

MATT@TTACK 08/04/22
peace out cub scout

[twitter.com]

Trending · #EatLawsonRich · 5,338 tweets

CNN @CNN · August 12

Lawson Rich, CEO of Emberi Group, now the richest man in the world, valued at $269 billion. (cnn.com)

1.2K Replies   **1.4K Retweets**   **942 Likes**

Tom Elvis Jedusor @qu33rdobby4311 · August 12
Replying to @CNN

Niiiiice #EatLawsonRich

---

8 Replies   **8 Retweets**   **12 Likes**

Syed Bashir @hesyedshesyed · August 12

Two hundred and sixty nine billion dollars. Truly an obscene number. No one *earns* that much money. They make it by exploiting workers, by not paying them what they're worth and convincing them they're doing them a favor by paying them at all. #EatLawsonRich

---

42 Replies   **65 Retweets**   **210 Likes**

Haisley Writes Words @hirehaisleystb · August 12

Ash got the ball rolling, but we can't depend on her to
#EatLawsonRich. I've worked at Feed Yourself (a subsidiary of
Emberi) for three years, and we've been starving for too long. It's
time to take what we're owed.

---

3 Replies   **2 Retweets**   **9 Likes**

Jeff Adams @defnotarushnbot2033 · August 12

How many of you depend on Emberi's companies to survive on
a daily basis? How many of you buy your groceries at FY, order
supplies with one day shipping through WE, or get your medicine
through SU?
How many of you are also tweeting to #EatLawsonRich?
I see you. You hypocrites.

Reply   **Retweet**   **1 Like**

Sienna Black @tortugablack227 · August 12
Replying to @BreitbartNews and @tortugablack227

and STILL be one of the richest people on the planet . . .Every
day that he decides NOT to do so is a conscious decision on his
part to let those people die.
#EATLAWSONRICH !!! (2/2)

---

2 Replies   **4 Retweets**   **15 Likes**

Sienna Black @tortugablack227 · August 12
Replying to @BreitbartNews

How is the NRA a worthy cause? How is donating to his OWN
CHARITY a worthy cause? Even if that weren't the case . . . That
10 million dollars is nothing to him. That'd be like someone who
makes 50K a year donating $1. Rich could end world hunger for
seven years($231bil) . . . (1/2)

---

4 Replies   **6 Retweets**   **20 Likes**

Mason Freeworth @amercanmason1955310 · August 12
Replying to @BreitbartNews

Truly Inspiring! Lawon started his business in his basement and
now look at what he's accomplished! What the hell are these
#eatlawsonrich folks on about! More like #EatLIKELawsonRich!
Steaks and champagne evvery day!

---

2 Replies   **Retweet**   **2 Likes**

Breitbart News @BreitbartNews · August 12

Lawson Rich, True American Patriot, named world's Richest Man
at 42, pledges $10 million to worthy causes (breitbart.com)

---

66 Replies   89 Retweets   399 Likes

A GUILLOTINE COST $1200
@gemmastarson1615 · August 12

Lawson Rich has to be next on the menu. Ash.
We need you. No one wants appetizers anymore.
We want the full course. #EatLawsonRich

---

6 Replies   1 Retweet   15 Likes

[newsbyconews.com]

Tobias Covington, richest man in the world, donates 90% of his wealth to charities
By Blaine Wilson | NEWSBYCO
Updated 8:09 AM ET, Mon Aug 12, 2022

(NEWSBYCO) — CEO of Covington Computing, Tobias Covington, shocked the world
Monday when he announced that he would be stepping down from the company he started and donating the vast majority of his wealth to over five thousand different charities across the world. Yesterday, Covington was worth $275 billion. Covington's staggering donation leaves him and his family with a modest $27.5 billion.

Covington started Covington Computing in his garage at 22, with only a minor cash injection from his parents, and has revolutionized the personal computer a dozen times over in the time since. When asked why he chose to abandon his wealth, Covington said . . .
Read more . . .

You need a subscription to continue reading this article.

Covering the news and helping citizens stay informed costs money. For journalists, for staff, for server costs, etc. Please support NEWSBYCO in order to stay informed.

Keep reading for $50 $5

Cancel any time. Seriously. If at any time you don't feel informed, or don't support our mission, you can cancel your support (as dictated by US law).

More Offers | Already a subscriber? **Sign in.**

Sponsored Stories You may like   Ad Content by Barabos

— 10 Tips For A Successful Backer Campaign That You'd Never Guess!

— Doctors Say These 8 Common Household Items Can Give You Cancer! Find Out Which!

— 9 Reasons You NEED Bootstrap Security To Protect Yourself And Your Assets!

— 16 Ways To Survive In The Gig Economy! You Won't Believe How Much These Apps Are Paying!

— 12 Lifehacks That Will Save You HUNDREDS Of Dollars A Year! You Won't Believe How Easy It Can Be!

Get in on the Conversation! (1,744)

PCInsanity24442 2m
@LtNutsNButts Yeah but it's not 250 billion dollars. That's the point. That number is not even misleading, it's just plain wrong.
Reply • Share • Report

LtNutsNButts201 4m

@PCInsanity24442 Wouldn't that still make him one of the biggest philanthropists in the world? Who cares what the numbers actually are?

Reply • Share • Report

PCInsanity24442 5m

And this news will tank CC's stock prices so his net worth will be worth substantially less by tomorrow . . . Either way, this article is misleading at best, and lying to us at worst.

Reply • Share • Report

PCInsanity24442 6m

Most of Covingtons net worth is in stock that's tied up in CC . . . does he plan on donating that stock, or is he simply donating 90% of his liquid cash? Because his net worth is 95% stock . . . Can you even donate stocks to charity?

Reply • Share • Report

34T5H1T81L5 8m

You have been spared, Tobias Covington. We know why you did this, and it's not out of the goodness of your heart. That doesn't negate the good you'll do with these donations but everyone else should take note that Ash FORCED these billionaire's hands, they didn't do it out of the kindness of their hearts.

Reply • Share • Report

Proud_____Patriot8201 10m

This makes it so that the biggest charity donation in the HISTORY of the world was done by an AMERICAN! USA! USA!

Reply • Share • Report

BethfullaGrace 10m

YOU EARNED THAT MONEY AND THEY DIDNTT!!!

YOURE JUST ENCOURAGING THEM TO BE LAZY AND TO HOPE THE BILLONARES BAIL THEM OUT!! THIS HURTS POOR PEOPLE, OPEN YOUR EYES!!
Reply • Share • Report

RickyBobby_22_1999 11m
Looking at the list of charities, and I'm not surprised to see 100% of the charities Ash listed on her last video on there. Tobias has obviously chosen a bunch of other charities to mask the fact that he's doing this under duress, but all of them seem legit, at first glance. AFAICT there's no shady business going on here. Good on you Covington! You're the first bil to see the writing on the wall.
Reply • Share • Report

Covington4Prez2024 12m
WOW . . . This move is DUMB AF!!!! You were the richest person in the world and you blew it!!! You gave it all up to LAWSON FREAKIN RICH!?!? I used to look up to you Tobias!!! No More!!!
Reply • Share • Report

PastorSmiley830111 15m
I know Tobias has said in the past that he's not a religious man . . . but THIS is an act of a man of God. Doesn't matter if he's explicit in his faith, only that his deeds match those exposed by the bible. Luke 12:33 "Sell your possessions, and give to the needy." We need more people who CLAIM to be men of faith to act like Tobias Covington!
Reply • Share • Report

SHOW MORE COMMENTS . . .

[reddit.com]

▲ 1,604 ▼

r/asheatstherich · Posted by u/eatlawsonrichnow ⊗ 7 months ago

Where's Ash?

It's been more than two months since the last ETR video. I know the Betsy Ragham vid got her banned from youtube but she said at the end of it that that wouldn't stop her from uploading vids in other places. So far this is the longest she's gone without uploading a video, and it worries me. I can't keep thinking that the only reason she'd stop making vids is that she's dead. She got shot taking down Ragham. Is it possible she died from complications from that? Or that she tried to take down someone bigger and their security got the better of her? Or some governmental agency or strike team found out her identity and took her out? I'm seriously freaking out here. Does anyone know what's going on with Ash?

SORT BY **BEST** ▼

terfscanfckofffff ⊗ 855 points · 7 months ago

There's two things that I think happened. She bit off more than she could chew with Ragham, and now the heat's too high to go after anyone right now. All of her potential targets are expecting her now, and are probably hiding out in literal bunkers with dozens of hired goons. She's scared them, which is good. Hell, Covington is *the* biggest fish out there and she scared him into giving away all his money.

Two, I think that since she kind of has her hands tied, that's why she put out the specials menu. She used the money she stole from the other courses and is putting it out into the world. It's not only about the biggest billionaires—the people on the specials menu are just as complicit in propping those people up. With potentially thousands of people going after those thousand contracts, it'll introduce a lot of chaos, and get a lot more done than if she tried to do the whole thing herself. And then when people are least expecting it, she can go after someone like Lawson Rich (nice username btw).

⊡ **Reply Share Report Save**

> **doctadatabase5983** ⊠ 701 points · 7 months ago
> That's a good point with the specials menu. Even if Ash never put out another video, she's changed the world and put a lot of this out into the forefront. We should have never let these people take advantage of us like this. Now they're scared. And they'll be scared for a long time even after Ash is dead.
> ⊡ **Reply Share Report Save**

> **eatlawsonrichnow** ⊠ 351 points · 7 months ago
> Nice username yourself. And yeah, I didn't think of that. They always thought they were invincible and now they know they're not. Ash has changed the world and we still don't even know her (his? their?) real name.
> ⊡ **Reply Share Report Save**

> **tahngyjumahnji2** ⊠ 89 points · 7 months ago
> Counter-Point: Ash had a mental breakdown live on youtube and has since been committed or done something stupid enough to get her killed. The Ragham video was instrumental in telling us who she really was.

⊟ **Reply Share Report Save**

terfscanfckofffff ⊠ 33 points · 7 months ago
We always knew who she was, the Ragham video
just got rid of the niceties. If you supported her
before then and have since changed your mind,
you're a hypocrite. This is life and death here.
Who gives a shit about Betsy Ragham.
⊟ **Reply Share Report Save**

tahngyjumahnji2 ⊠ 11 points · 7 months ago
I never supported her. I just think people were
duped by the cutesy recipe videos she posted, even
though she's been upfront all along that she was
murdering people. Look at **this** photo and tell me
that that's a person you support. I'll wait. I'd rather
be a hypocrite than a cultist. Because that's what
this bullshit is. A cult.
⊟ **Reply Share Report Save**

atypicalpenguin00229 ⊠ 22 points · 7 months ago
Can't take anyone with a slur in their username seriously.
You can go fuck right off.
⊟ **Reply Share Report Save**

mediumrawrstake88 ⊠ 8 points · 7 months ago
i'm sorry if I'm being stupid about this, but
where's the slur?
⊟ **Reply Share Report Save**

atypicalpenguin00229 ⊠ 2 points · 7 months
ago
Terf. Terf is a slur.
⊟ **Reply Share Report Save**

mediumrawrstake88 ⊠ 6 points • 7 months ago
what the fuck is a Terf
⊟ **Reply Share Report Save**

> **terfscanfckofffff** ⊠ 5 points • 7 months ago
> Trans-Exclusionary Radical Feminist. Basically people who deny that trans women have a place in the feminist movement.
> ⊟ **Reply Share Report Save**

>> **atypicalpenguin00229** ⊠ -1 point • 7 months ago
>> There are two genders. Denial doesn't change science. Read a fucking book sometime dingus.
>> ⊟ **Reply Share Report Save**

> **terfscanfckofffff** ⊠ 7 points • 7 months ago
> There isn't one. Penguin is the type of person that argues that "boomer" is a slur. It's descriptive. And in this case, it's a label for a hate group, who are angry that they're being labelled as such.
> ⊟ **Reply Share Report Save**

battypatsysince1987 ⊠ 553 points • 7 months ago
Don't care anymore. Ash went too far with the Betsy Ragham video. It totally tarnished her legacy and anyone who still supports her is a psychopath. Cancel the bitch.
⊟ **Reply Share Report Save**

> **billionaireburger** ⊠ 761 points • 7 months ago
> ok bootlicker

a

⊡ **Reply Share Report Save**

battypatsysince1987 ⊠ 141 points · 7 months ago

What the fuck did you just fucking say about me, you little bitch? I'll have you know I graduated top of my class in the Navy Seals, and I've been involved in numerous secret raids on Al-Quaeda, and I have over 300 confirmed kills. I am trained in gorilla warfare and I'm the top sniper in the entire US armed forces.

You are nothing to me but just another target. I will wipe you the fuck out with precision the likes of which has never been seen before on this Earth, mark my fucking words. You think you can get away with saying that shit to me over the Internet? Think again, fucker. As we speak I am contacting my secret network of spies across the USA and your IP is being traced right now so you better prepare for the storm, maggot. The storm that wipes out the pathetic little thing you call your life. You're fucking dead, kid. I can be any-where, anytime, and I can kill you in over seven hundred ways, and that's just with my bare hands. Not only am I extensively trained in unarmed combat, but I have access to the entire arsenal of the United States Marine Corps and I will use it to its full extent to wipe your miserable ass off the face of the continent, you little shit. If only you could have known what unholy retribution your little "clever" comment was about to bring down upon you, maybe you would have held your fucking tongue. But you couldn't, you didn't, and now you're paying the price, you goddamn idiot.

I will shit fury all over you and you will drown in
it. You're fucking dead, kiddo.

☐ **Reply Share Report Save**

> **yallquedayeehawbonnie** ⊠ 78 points · 7 months
> ago
> Can't believe this copypasta is still going around, its
> older than the internet itself
> ☐ **Reply Share Report Save**

> > **battypatsysince1987** ⊠ 51 points · 7 months
> > ago
> > What is dead may never die.
> > ☐ **Reply Share Report Save**

transmetgonzospidrrt ⊠ 282 points · 7 months ago
Can't cancel a revolution. Ash isn't some racist comedian
that made a shitty joke. Ash is the guillotine, Ash is the
trumpets sounding the rapture, Ash is life. Get ready
bootlicker, cuz your ass is next on the line.

☐ **Reply Share Report Save**

> **tahngyjumahnji2** ⊠ 100 points · 7 months ago
> Earlier in the thread I literally called Ash's follow-
> ing a cult. Thanks for proving me right.
> ☐ **Reply Share Report Save**

> > **transmetgonzospidrrt** ⊠ 88 points · 7 months
> > ago
> > Cults end up killing themselves in the end. Ash is
> > the one who'll set us free.
> > ☐ **Reply Share Report Save**

> > > **tahngyjumahnji2** ⊠ 23 points · 7 months
> > > ago

Exactly what someone in a cult would say.
⮌ **Reply Share Report Save**

slaphappytv⊠ 440 points · 7 months ago
Didn't Ash say she had a dead man's switch? I always thought that
if she died she'd publish a bunch of incriminating info that she
found along with donating all the stolen money. We haven't seen
anything like that yet so I wouldn't be too worried.
⮌ **Reply Share Report Save**

> **tomnookdaddy42** ⊠ 150 points · 7 months ago
> I didn't think about that. Good point. Also, did we ever
> found out HOW she got the money from all the people
> she killed? How she got access to those bank accounts,
> and how she was able to transfer the funds to herself
> without authorities catching her?
> ⮌ **Reply Share Report Save**

> > **Slaphappytv** ⊠ 44 points · 7 months ago
> > Not that I've seen, and I've been keeping up with
> > the situation pretty well.
> > Maybe it's better that we don't know how she does
> > it. So she can keep doing it for whoever she takes
> > down next.
> > ⮌ **Reply Share Report Save**

> > **reapandtar2016** ⊠ 5 points · 7 months ago
> > I still think the whole thing is a ruse and she's
> > laundering the money for these people to avoid
> > taxes . . . or else, you're right, how did she get that
> > money?
> > ⮌ **Reply Share Report Save**

> > > **tomnookdaddy42** ⊠ 15 points · 7 months ago

Did you see the Betsy Ragham video?

⊡ **Reply Share Report Save**

aenaemananthema ⊠ 33 points · 7 months ago

Are we sure that the specials menu WASN'T her dead man's switch . . .?

⊡ **Reply Share Report Save**

    slaphappytv⊠ 551 points · 7 months ago

    Shit, I didn't even think of that. Hope not.

    ⊡ **Reply Share Report Save**

    aenaemananthema ⊠ 1 point · 6 months ago

    called it

    ⊡ **Reply Share Report Save**

Episode 5

Lawson Rich and the Dead Man's Switch

[Editor's Note: For Ash's past videos, I transcribed her speech without editorializing. This was done because she was talking directly to the camera, narrating her actions, and I thought that the transcription provided enough context without adding anything myself. This video is different. There are multiple people speaking in the video, there are parts without dialogue that are crucial to understanding what's going on, there are visual elements that are not conveyed through speech, and for that reason I have decided to format this part of the record differently.

The unaltered text is still Ash. The text in italics is written by me.

I've tried to be as impartial as I can, as I thought it was important for me to be merely a provider of context rather than a voice in the narrative itself. But now I've decided to inject just a little bit of myself into the narrative. As a bit of flavor. Apologies if it doesn't land.]

If you're watching this, then I'm dead.

Ash is sitting at her desk, the same one she sat at during the Eat the Rich videos. She's sitting where she sat and explained to us why the people she killed deserved to die. Her hair is knotted, clumped, and her makeup is smeared. A ring of blood surrounds her mouth. The room is littered with debris: porcelain plates shattered on the floor, glass from windows that were shattered inwards, body parts of David or Harry or Betsy or whoever. Blood splatter takes up the entire back wall. It is unclear why, if she is using deepfake tech to mask her face, she wouldn't choose a more composed image.

I've thought about this for a long time. I thought about this before I even did the David White video. I thought: Am I Ash? Is Ash a construct, or an idea? Is Ash the revolution personified? It was very important to me. I didn't want my own face or my own name associated with Ash, that was the only thing I knew for sure. I wasn't doing this to get famous. I'm not doing this to be famous. That's why I hid my face. That's why I'm still wearing the mask, even in this video, even after I've died.

Things start to change. The changes are almost imperceptible. You don't notice them as they happen. If you skip from the beginning of the video to the end, the changes are night and day, but if you try to focus in on them as they happen you're barely able to pinpoint exactly what changes when.

The thing I was waffling on was this. If I died eating the rich—and it was always a possibility, this is dangerous work—if I died, then what happens next? Do I drop off the face of the earth, and my work lives on through the actions of those I've inspired? Do I live on in the Backer benefactors and the bootlicker bashers and in the hearts and minds of blah and blah and blah? Do I choose a successor, and have them use my face to continue my work, making sure that Ash lives forever and is a perpetual boogeyman to the rich? Or do I create a dead man's switch, record a video to go along with it, to tell everyone what happened? What purpose can I have in dying if I don't know when that will be?

The blood stains on the wall and the ring of blood around Ash's mouth start to fade. Debris begins to disappear from the background. A piece of glass here, a leg or an arm there. Ash's hair goes from matted and knotted to straight and of a style. The smeared makeup on Ash's face reverts to what it must have looked like right after she applied it.

This is what I settled on. I've mentioned the dead man's switch before. But it's not just one switch. It's two. Tomorrow night, I'm going to try and take down Lawson Rich. If I succeed, I plan to take him alive. I don't know what I'll do to him. That comes later. I have a lot of ideas. Some of them thematic, some of them practical but more painful. We'll see.

But if I fail, and it's highly likely that I will, I'm recording the entire thing. I'm recording what happens tonight and streaming the video as it happens to a server . . . somewhere. You don't need to know where the server is. Just know that if the video is recorded and I don't execute a script on my computer by tomorrow night, then the first dead man's switch gets flipped. Ash's Specials Menu.

Everyone notices the changes in the video at a different point. No one notices them right away, but you might have noticed it by this point, you might not notice it at all. We've always known that Ash's face isn't real, that it's a mask, but now you know that nothing she's presented is real. Her living room, her kitchen, her physical form. She is not a magician, but you have to actively convince yourself of that as you watch her living room reconstruct itself before your very eyes. As you watch Ash go from the mess she was at the end of the Betsy Ragham video back to the way she looked at the beginning of the David White video.

Over a thousand contracts against the enablers, against the supporters, against the sycophants of the world that are technically rich; they're richer than we'll ever be, but they'll never be as filthy rich as Betsy and Lawson. They're the bootlicker upper class, the politicians, the ones with aspirations to ascend, the ones that sell us out and are the buffer between people like us and people like Lawson. You'll take them out and I'll pay you with Betsy's money. Everything's automated; everything is in place and everyone can get paid without any input from me. That's what happens if I die.

And then you begin to wonder, much like Ash did earlier: How much of Ash is a construct? How much of Ash is the person behind Ash, and how much is a narrative? Was the meltdown during the Betsy Ragham video real? Was she actually shot, or was that added to make the story have stakes? Did she actually take those painkillers? Did she really slit Ragham's throat and drink her spurting blood? Is she a woman? Is she a person? Is she many people? Is Ash an avatar or a person? You do not know. But you wonder.

For the second part, you need to work for it. If 10 percent of those contracts are filled—a little more than a hundred—this video is released. If you're watching this video, then people are eating from the specials menu. And that's good. The wealth is being redistributed. That's good too.

And if things go sideways, this video might not even make it to you. People like Lawson Rich have a way of hiding their tracks and staying unseen. I have a contingency plan. A "blink and you'll miss it" type plan. See if you can spot it.

Ash's living room is spotless. She looks perfect. Impeccable. But that's not really her. It was always a mask, but you fooled yourself. Who is Ash? Maybe we'll never know. But it's a question we'll be asking long after all this is over. Who is Ash Whatever?

It's time to sleep. Big day tomorrow. If you're watching this, then I'm proud of you. You needed to earn this, and you did. You needed to eat and keep eating if you wanted to take down Lawson Rich. But that's not enough. Eat and gorge yourself and never be satiated. Keep eating until there's nothing left. There is only right now, friends. Eat.

The scene cuts to another. You don't recognize what it is right away, and it only lasts for a second or two. It cuts away again before you can fully grasp it. You press the left arrow key on your keyboard, rewinding the video five seconds. You pause it when the transition happens. The camera this time is pointed skyward. It's night. Black lines crisscrossing like veins across the night sky. The camera's flash illuminates them. Tree branches. It's unclear what the camera is focusing on. There's something stuck to one of the branches. A bump. It flashes once, twice, but maybe it's the reflection from another light source somewhere.

The video cuts again. To a room filled with people this time, but the video is not centered on Ash. The video is not from a webcam in a living room. Or wherever Ash was before. It is from her point of view. You might think it was a mounted GoPro, but what you learn later is that it is not. She is in a room that looks more like a bunker than anything else. There are rows of guns mounted to the walls and neon-blue lights illuminating the space and eight other individuals crowded together. An armory. They are arming themselves. It looks like they're preparing for war.

"Ash," one of the individuals says. His back is to her. He's wearing SWAT gear or maybe it's military or maybe it's black ops. It doesn't matter. Maybe it's a man; it's unclear. The voice is garbled. It's being filtered. The person is just that: a person. Man or woman, it doesn't matter. They're inspecting the weapon they're holding, and they don't turn to look at her. "Where do you get this shit?"

I know some people. I have friends other than you.

Her voice disembodied, coming from behind the camera. The only other time we've seen her is when she's addressing us and the disconnect is striking.

"Yeah," they say. They laugh. *"I guess you do. Are they the same people that made the masks?"*

No, Sam, they're different people.

Sam turns around. They don't have a face. Ash's deepfake tech is at work here, but instead of giving Sam a random face, someone we won't know but swear we recognize all the same, she's taken their face away. Swirls and artifacting features and blurred lines. It's like a horror movie. Like something out of a nightmare. Beneath the mask, you can tell the person is smiling.

"I never asked," they say, *"because I trust you. But was this whole Ash thing your idea? Or did someone put you up to it?"*

Ash reaches out her right hand and places it on Sam's shoulder.

We've known each other a long time, Sam. What do you think?

You can't see Sam's eyes but you can tell they're meeting Ash's. They're studying her. Really considering the answer.

"It's just you," Sam says.

That's right. I have connections and I have help, but the idea was all me. Who else would be stupid enough to do this shit?

"It was always going to be you," Sam says.

No. It was always going to be someone. It just happened to be me.

Sam nods. They turn around and look back at their weapon.

"This is some sci-fi shit," they say. The other people in the bunker are still suiting up. Another figure turns around, not Sam, and walks over to Ash. Even though you can't see their face, even though it's all shapes and swirls of darkness and blurred edges, you can tell it's different than Sam's.

"You sure about this?" they say. Their voice a different tone than Sam's, but still androgynous. Mechanical.

Yeah, Jamie, I'm sure.

"Like you were sure about the Ragham video?"

Ash's camera moves visibly away from Jamie, as if she's taken aback. She steadies herself and exhales deeply, loud and echoing in the camera's microphone. Wherever that is.

I was trying something.

"It didn't work," Jamie says.

No, it didn't work.

"It was actually kind of insensitive to people with substance abuse issues," Jamie says. Their face, somehow you can tell that they're not looking at Ash. They're not meeting her gaze.

I understand. I'm sorry.

"And it turned off a lot of people to the cause," Jamie says.

I know. It was a mistake. I should have listened to you.

You notice that every few seconds the feed flashes black for a moment. This persists throughout the entire video, but it's so subtle that you might miss it if you weren't paying close attention. You ask yourself: Why?

"And you're sure about this?"

This was always the endgame. How many times have we talked about this? I need us on the same page, Jamie.

"You're right," Jamie says. "It's just nerves." Their face still looking at the ground. Their fingers twiddling and fidgeting. You ask yourself: This is Ash's team?

I don't believe you. You've never been nervous before. Remember that mission in—

"No identifying information. You're still recording, right?"

Shit, yeah. I forgot. It's easy to forget I have this thing in me.

In me, she says. Not on me. In me. What does she mean by that?

"I'll get over it when we're in the shit."

Yeah, you always do.

Another blurred face walks up to Jamie and Ash.

"You guys ready?"

Let's do this fucking thing.

The scene cuts again. To a close-up of dirt this time. Like the last interstitial, it only lasts for a second or two. Ash has something in her left hand and she pushes it into the dirt. Whatever it is, it's beeping softly. The dirt muffles it. Silences it. You ask yourself: What is she doing?

The scene cuts again. Ash and her team are outside. Five hundred yards or so away from a house. You might recognize it as Lawson Rich's house in Connecticut, you might not. You correct yourself. It's not a house. It's a compound. How are they going to get inside? They're at a tree line. The forest that borders Rich's compound. Ash looks at her watch.

One minute.

Jamie turns to Ash. She's shaking. You ask yourself again: This is Ash's team? The ones who kidnapped and killed David White, Harry Cadejo, Rocco Mann, and Betsy Ragham?

You good, Jamie?

"Yeah," Jamie says. "What's the timeline again?"

Ash checks her watch again.

Fifty seconds.

"How many did you plant?" Jamie says.

Three. Max just drove a drone over the house and dropped one on the roof.

The camera looks up. You see a speck in the sky fly off into the night. The movement of the camera isn't smooth. It jerks from side to side and moves to whoever's talking. It's as if it's Ash's actual POV, what her eyes see, and not attached to a helmet or her head somehow.

"Why are we doing this again?" another says. "The video's streaming to the server regardless. We don't need these hoppers."

It's a back-up plan. Just in case.

"Ash knows what she's doing," Jamie says.

"Either we get out of this or we don't. I don't understand why we're leaving this tech behind."

The dead man's switch is important. There has to be contingencies in place.

"Just have faith," Jamie says. "No one's planning on dying, but you know that that's a possibility."

Hopefully we don't need it. Hopefully it's a backup plan that stays a backup plan.

The lights in Rich's compound go dark. The lights illuminating his vast, impossibly large yard go dark. Presumably, the security system inside the house is also disabled.

I knew Max would come through.

"Max knows their shit," Sam says.

Smart homes. You'd think after Betsy they'd stay somewhere with actual physical security.

"He might have a panic room," Jamie says.

That's why I have this.

Ash gestures to her rucksack.

I'm kind of looking forward to using it.

The scene cuts again. Ash's team moves through a room. The inside of Rich's compound. It looks like a TV set. Like pictures you'd see on a real estate website. Not like a real place. A place you might imagine yourself living, but you know deep down, you will never live in a place like this. This kind of place isn't for you. It's an impossibility. Only people like Rich live here.

Everything is made of glass or colored gold. Gaudy. Tacky. The ceilings are higher than your house. Ash aims her hand towards the ceiling. Not holding anything, just gesturing with an open hand. Something is propelled towards the ceiling, shot out of her wrist like a projectile in a video game. It's another one of the things she planted outside. It sticks to the ceiling, inconspicuous. No one looks up in a house like this. No one looks around and appreciates what they have. They take it for granted.

Another one.

"Kitchen next," Sam says. Their voices a whisper. "Then to the bedroom."

"This looks different than the blueprints we got," Jamie says, whispering in turn.

Yeah. But just a little different. Not enough to change the plan.

"Not enough to change the plan," Sam says.

The scene cuts again, to a kitchen. The kitchen is bigger than your apartment. There are two fridges. A wall of refrigerated coolers with glass doors like a 7-11. A wall of stoves. Two islands punctuating the middle of the space. Ash points her hand at one of the fridges. Something lodges itself behind the fridge.

There's the second one.

"Let's go upstairs," one of them says. Someone whose name we haven't learned yet.

Yeah, we're burning time. Let's get him and get the fuck out of here.

The scene cuts again. Ash's team is ascending a spiral staircase. Ash leads the pack, and she looks back every few seconds to check in on her team. They make their way down a hallway that's wider than your bedroom. They make their way to a door. A door that opens in the middle and has golden knobs that cost more than your wedding ring. Three of Ash's team stand in front of the door, making hand gestures to the others that indicate that they're going to breach Rich's bedroom. Ash is the furthest away from the door. The others nod in agreement. Everyone except Jamie. Ash's camera nods in agreement.

"This is wrong," Jamie says. "It feels wrong."

Go.

The three nearest the door open the door and the others follow. Jamie and Ash move into the room last. The room is massive, bigger than the office filled with cubicles in which you work. There is a bed in the center of the room. It's bigger than your car. There is a figure under the sheets. The sheets rise and fall; the figure is breathing, deep in sleep.

Remember, we want him alive.

"That's not him," Jamie says. "That's not—"

Everything happens very quickly. And most of it is not caught on the video you're watching. But if you rewind a few seconds and pause, you can look at the figure sleeping in the bed. It's too small to be Lawson Rich. Rich is six feet four inches tall, a beast of a man. Muscular and fit from his access to the best superfoods and best personal trainers. The figure in the bed is small. Maybe a woman. Not his wife: she is taller than average as well. A random woman, perhaps. It doesn't matter. You never find out who is sleeping in the bed.

Gunfire. It happens before you can register what is happening. Ash's team doesn't have time to react. There's the sound of multiple hostiles firing on Ash's team and the room lights up with muzzle flashes like it's been peppered by lightning. Jamie spins around to aim at the man who appeared as if by magic to their right, but they are taken down. Sam spins the other way and doesn't even get off a shot before they are hit and fall to the ground. Ash aims her gun and presses the trigger, but all you hear is clicks.

Shit. What the f—?

Ash stops trying to fire her gun. Her right hand goes to her throat, out of view of the camera. She falls to her knees. The camera looks left and right, back and forth, wildly panning around the room. There's ten men in similar gear to Ash's team checking the bodies on the floor. Ash slumps onto her back as one of the men walks over to her and stands over her body.

"Oh, what I wouldn't give to put a bullet between this bitch's eyes," the man says.

"Boss wants her alive," another says.

"Yeah," the first one says. "But how easy would it be to tell him she got caught in the line of fire? That she didn't make it?"

"You want to be the one to tell him that?" a third one says. "I'm not going to lie to that crazy son of a bitch. You want to end up like her?"

"He's watching us," the second one says. "There's no way he's not watching this."

The camera aimed upward, you see three men standing over Ash's body. The camera gets fuzzy and the top and bottom of the screen start to go black. Like Ash's eyes are closing. The camera focuses for a moment on the endlessly high ceiling of Rich's bedroom. In the corner, there is a security camera. The red light flashes. Ash lifts her hand, with difficulty, aiming her wrist at the camera. Something shoots from her wrist and lodges itself at the base of the camera. Right on target. The man closest to Ash's right hand kicks at her wrist with his foot a moment after she shoots.

"You missed," he said.

"Stupid bitch," the second one says.

The feed goes black. The blackness encroaches from the top and bottom of the screen. But the feed continues. Silence. A slight hiss of static. You can infer that the scene does cut at some point, but it's only in retrospect. There *is a time jump. You hear voices, but the screen is still black. You can assume by this point that somehow Ash is recording what she's actually seeing. Maybe by cameras embedded in contact lenses. But you remember what she said earlier: It's easy to forget I have this thing in me. In me. Not on me. Not something she's wearing. She said* in *me.*

"You searched her things," *a voice says. You recognize the voice.* Lawson Rich.

"Yes, sir," *another voice says. A woman.*

The woman's voice is unnerving. It makes the hairs on your neck stand up and something feels off about it. Like it's not real. It sounds . . . familiar.

"And?" *Rich says.*

"Their gear is from Citizen One. Not available to the public. Not even something the public would be aware of."

Citizen One. The pharmaceutical company?

"The same guns our men have?"

"Similar to what our men have." *She must have misspoke. The guns came from Citizen One? The same Citizen One manned by the now dead Rocco Mann?*

"We figured," *Rich says.* "The signal jammer was able to target their guns, which gave us the edge. That was good thinking on your part."

"The morgue technician that examined Ragham's men told us as much. Not exactly, but I was able to infer. It was an educated guess."

"You never guess, Emma," *Rich says.* "Give yourself more credit than that."

That's it. You recognize the voice. Emma, the virtual assistant. One of Emberi's most prolific products. But . . . the way she's talking is not the way an Emma talks. It sounds almost human. Is Emma's voice based off of this person? Any other explanation starts to sound like science fiction.

"She's awake, Mr. Rich," *the not-Emma says.*

"How can you tell?" *Rich says.* "Not that I don't believe you."

"Elevated heart rate," *the not-Emma says.* "An increased respiratory rate. A lack of rapid eye movement."

Ash's eyes open. The video feed opens from a horizontal center line and fills the screen. Ash is sitting in a chair and Lawson is standing in front of her. *The room is dark. There is a solitary lightbulb hanging from the ceiling. The floors are wet concrete and exposed pipes line the walls. This does not look like a room in Lawson Rich's compound. It looks like a second location. It looks like someone designed it with an explicit instruction: make it look like a room you would torture someone in.*

"Wakey, wakey," Rich says. "Eggs and bakey."

Cute. But you're not as charming as you think you are.

Ash's eyes glance downward and you see her arms and legs are tied to a metal chair. Her legs are bare and the camera jerks upwards as she remembers she's recording. Her skin is darker than it was in the Eat the Rich videos.

Were you just talking to an Emma?

"Not an Emma," Rich says. "The Emma."

There is no one else in the room with Lawson Rich and Ash. Ash cranes her neck and the camera moves with it. You see two large flat-screen monitors hanging on the wall behind Rich. Their screens are black, but they're on, and each one is segmented into nine equal sections separated by white lines.

Who were you talking to?

"I told you," Rich says. "Emma."

Say whatever you want to say, man. I'm livestreaming this to the entire fucking internet right now. You're fucked.

A smile creeps onto Rich's face, but he doesn't laugh. He doesn't even chuckle. You are unsure of whether he's even capable.

"No, you're not," he says. "But you already knew that. You were listening."

You said there was a signal jammer.

"That's right," he says.

He starts to pace the room. There's puddles on the floor and he makes no effort to sidestep them. His shoes look like they cost more than you've made in the last year and he's getting mud all over them. He doesn't care.

My team and I were all wearing GPS trackers. If I don't hit the dead man's switch by morning, they'll activate and the world will know we're here.

Rich stops pacing. He adjusts the cuffs of his shirt. First one, and then the other. He looks Ash in her eyes, right into the camera, as if he's seeing you there.

You were. And now those trackers are on their way to Qatar.

Qatar. Do you know where Qatar is? Somewhere in the Middle East, right? You pause the video. You google it. Qatar borders Saudi Arabia. You feel ignorant for not knowing it offhand. You resume the video.

Why am I naked?

"This isn't an interview," Rich says. The smirk has left his face. "Who do you think has the upper hand here?"

I'm just wondering if this is like, a sex thing.

Rich grimaces. He takes a step back from Ash, as if the mere suggestion offends him. To you, it seems like a valid question.

"Don't be absurd," Rich says. "It's a safety precaution. I don't know what sort of tech you stole from CO. Socks embedded with lockpicks. Underwear that . . . shoots out lasers or some fucking thing. Mann always came up with the most bizarre prototypes."

You hear Ash breathe out a sigh of relief. She's willing to die for the cause. Anything else . . . well, what Rich said is somewhat of a relief.

Funny you say that. I have a bomb embedded in my small intestine. Voice activated. Let me go and I won't say the catchphrase.

Rich sighs. He looks like he's losing his patience.

"No, you don't," he says. "I expected more from you, Ash. Can we stop this charade, please?"

Ash pauses. She takes in a deep breath and then screams. She screams loud into the room and it echoes, the echoes overlapping one another. Nothing happens. Ash starts to laugh. It turns into a cackle. The sound echoes and overlaps in the enclosed space.

You didn't even flinch.

"Are you done?" Rich says.

Let's get this over with.

Rich turns around, exposing his back to Ash.

"Emma, initiate the call," Rich says.

"Calling," Emma says. Her voice comes from the monitor's speakers.

Emma, call the police.

"Emma only responds to me," Rich says. "But nice try."

One by one, faces appear in the segmented sections on the dual monitors.

They are heavily backlit and the faces are darkened to the point of anonymity. Each face is accompanied by a number. One through eighteen. You try to make out the details of even one face, to try and identify them, but it's almost as if they are being disguised by the same technology Ash used for her team. Their faces are purposefully vague. When every section is filled, Lawson Rich addresses them.

"This is her," Rich says.

"Of course she'd come after you," the face in the section labelled "Three" says.

"Why is she naked?" Five says.

"Are you planning on doing a . . . sex thing?" Eleven says.

"Of course not," Rich says. "She had CO tech. I was trying to be careful. You never know with Mann."

"He's right," Eighteen says. "You never knew with Mann."

"Guy is just as esoteric," Fourteen says. "We should keep an eye on him."

"Who?" Six says.

"Which guy?" Twelve says.

Guy Capps, you idiots.

"Who?" Six says.

CO's CFO.

"Oh," Six says. Even through the face masking tech you can hear the embarrassment.

"She doesn't look like what we expected," Eleven says.

"Exactly what I was thinking," Ten says.

I was masking my face, you dumb fucks.

"How do we know it's actually her?" Nine says.

You guys are fucked, you know that?

"She and a team of eight highly trained individuals infiltrated my house," Rich says.

"She might be one of those . . . what do you call them?" Nine says.

"Copycats," Eleven says.

All of you. All of you are fucked.

"She was fully outfitted with CO tech," Rich says. "Who else would have access?"

"Do you think Guy is making a play?" One says.

"He doesn't have the balls," Three says.

I wasn't lying about the dead man's switch.

"What's she talking about, Rich?" Four says.

"Didn't you watch her videos?" Rich says.

"Too violent for my tastes," Four says.

Rich is preoccupied talking to the screens. He has not looked back at Ash in minutes. You see Ash struggling against her ties. She tries to be quiet.

"Says the war profiteer," Fifteen says.

"I sell white phosphorus," Four says, "but I don't have to watch it being used."

"The violence is implied," Eight says.

"I don't like to think about it," Four says.

Water drips from the pipes on to the exposed concrete. The dripping sound is maddening. Ash looks down at her ties. Still quietly struggling. You see a row of parallel horizontal scars on her thighs. A deeper, more pronounced crisscrossing of scars across both wrists. The scars are faded. They are old. But you see them.

"How cute," Eleven says.

"She thinks she can escape," Seventeen says.

"Should we be worried about this dead man's switch?" Thirteen says.

You should be. You won't be, you won't be until it's too late, but you should be now.

"What sort of information could she have gotten already?" Twelve says.

"It's impossible to tell," Rich says.

He still has not looked back at Ash. You don't think it's because he feels guilty looking at her. You think it's because he considers her a nuisance and not a threat. Better to not even acknowledge her.

"Should we be worried?" Thirteen says.

"No, I don't think so," Rich says.

Wait a second. White phosphorus. Is that you, Ulrich?

"What?" Four says. "I—No."

"She made you," Five says.

"Maybe it is her," Eighteen says.

"What did we agree on?" Rich says. "Ten? Each?"

"I'm not paying you a goddamn cent until we confirm her identity," One says.

I know the answer already. I'm not stupid. But just so that none of you can say I didn't warn you—

"Shut her up," Ulrich says. "Please."

Let me go and the switch doesn't get flipped.

Rich turns around. His face is stoic. No remorse or disgust or even anger. Maybe . . . maybe impatience. But that is all.

"You're not stupid, Ash. You know how this ends."

"Before you do anything," Seven says, "we need to disable the dead man's switch. Just in case."

My only regret . . .

"Shut her up," Nine says. "Gag her if you have to."

There's just so many politicians I wanted to kill. It's a shame I didn't have the time.

"We'll get her to talk," Rich says. "We have all the time in the world."

No. You don't.

You hear a crunch. Or a snap. Ash bit down on something. The camera shakes as Ash convulses. Her eyelids close and the view of Rich and the monitors disappears.

"What's happening?" a voice says.

"Goddamn suicide pill," Rich says. "I need to fire whoever searched her."

"Should we be worried?" a voice says. Probably Thirteen.

"I'm still not convinced that she's Ash," another voice says.

You do not know who is talking. All of the modulated voices sound the same, and without the monitors to inform you, they could all be the same person.

"She knew it was you, Ulrich," a voice says. "She could have found that out from Mann."

"I knew we couldn't trust that motherfucker," Ulrich says.

"You never know with Mann," Rich says.

"You never knew with Mann," a voice says.

"And the dead man's switch?" a voice says.

"Nothing she knew could possibly hurt us," a voice says.

"Should we be worried?" a voice says. Probably Thirteen.

"I guess we'll find out soon enough," Rich says.

A quick google search tells you suicide pills were common throughout World War II to prevent captured spies from leaking their country's secrets to the enemy. Cyanide was the chemical commonly used. Cyanide poisoning takes two to five minutes to kill the poisoned person and it is extremely painful. The few minutes that it takes the person to die feels like an eternity.

One last snuff film. Ash didn't get to eat the rich in her last video, but she provided you with the tools to do it yourself. One last recipe. You know now that the dead man's switch released the bounties on Ash's Specials Menu. Not incriminating evidence on the eighteen faceless voices in the video showing her death. But maybe, just maybe, it will be enough to take down Lawson Rich.

Thankfully, you are not subjected to the full death of Ash Whatever. The audio cuts out and the video feed is dark for a full thirty seconds. Then a URL flashes on the screen.

[twitter.com]

← Trends

Trending in United States
#RIPAsh
145.1K Tweets

Trending in United States
Lawson Rich
Trending with: Emberi CEO

Trending in United States
#EattheRich
3.2M Tweets

Trending in United States
#EatLawsonRich
Trending with: #ArrestLawsonRich

Trending in United States
#CantStopCaturday
3,817 Tweets

Trending in United States
#13shouldbeworried
2,123 Tweets

Trending in United States
Emberi
Trending with: Citizen One

Trending in United States
#DumpEmberiStock
5,401 Tweets

Trending in United States
#IfICouldDeepFakeId
2,455 Tweets

Trending in United States
Ash Whatever
Trending with: Eat the Rich

Trending in United States
#DontTrustEmma
11.4K Tweets

Trending in United States
#YouShouldThinkAboutIt
2,209 Tweets

Trending in United States
Ulrich K⊠nig
Trending with: White Phosphorus

Trending in United States
Guy Capps
Trending with: doesn't have the balls

[reddit.com]

▲ 2,087 ▼
r/asheatstherich · Posted by u/destroy_all_emmas46 ⊗ 7 months ago

Can someone explain to me how the dead man's switch worked?

What were the things that Ash planted outside Lawson's house? What did she shoot at the security guard right before she was taken? Where was her camera hidden if Rich stripped her naked and she was searched? How did the video even get released when Rich kept talking about signal jammers and GPS trackers sent to Qatar and why did the video only get released a month later after Rich had plenty of time to destroy the evidence? Is Ash actually dead or is she framing Rich for her own murder? What is this specials menu people keep talking about? I'm so confused I feel like I can't even follow the plot of this whole thing and I feel stupid for even asking so many questions but I want to understand.

SORT BY **BEST** ▼

bestofashwhatever ⊗ 1,501 points · 7 months ago
Well, that's a lot of questions, and most of them don't have clear cut answers, but I'll do my best. A lot of this is speculation so take it with a grain of salt.

1. *What were the things that Ash planted outside Lawson's house? What did she shoot at the security guard right before she was taken?*

2. We don't know. What we can assume is that whatever she shot

at the security guard is the same kind of tech she planted outside the house. My best guess is that whatever she planted there helped her release the video despite Rich's signal jammers. She called them "hoppers," but I've never heard that term before.

3. *Where was her camera hidden if Rich stripped her naked and she was searched?*

   Again, we don't know for sure. At several times during the video "stolen tech from CO" is mentioned and also Ash says "its easy to forget I have this thing in me". People have speculated that she was wearing some kind of camera embedded in a contact lens, but other people have pointed out that she didn't say "it's easy to forget I'm wearing this thing". She said "in me". Personally I think she had a camera surgically implanted in her eye to ensure the camera stayed rolling, but neither kind of technology actually exists (that we know of) so it's hard to say.

4. *How did the video even get released when Rich kept talking about signal jammers?*

   My best guess is, and again, this is pure speculation, but the hoppers she planted outside had storage capacity and the ability to upload the video to a private server. Her camera recorded locally and after she was kidnapped/after she died, Rich turned off the signal jammers because he no longer thought they were necessary. Then the video was uploaded from her camera to the devices outside to a private server. Rich thought he beat her so he got sloppy.

5. *Why did the video only get released a month later after Rich had plenty of time to destroy the evidence?*

   People seem split on this. Some people think that the delay in the release of the video helps Rich, because like you said, he got to destroy evidence. Others say that having a month between Ash's death and the release of the video damns Rich further, because he can't claim he killed her in self-defense. He killed her (well, technically she killed herself, but under duress) and disposed of the body and never went to the police. Ash said herself she wanted people to "work for it", presumably to ensure that some amount of the contracts were fulfilled. Who knows?

6. *Is Ash actually dead or is she framing Rich for her own murder?*

    I think she's really dead. I think she was willing to die for the cause and killed herself as a "fuck you" to Lawson Rich. Which is a badass way to go, I think. Either way, this is the last we're going to see of Ash. Because if she did frame him, reappearing suddenly would exonerate him.

7. *What is this specials menu people keep talking about?*

    See **this link** for a detailed rundown of what the specials menu was/is. u/billionaireburger did a really good job with that post.

I hope this helps, even a little bit. I know most of my answers were "we don't know, here's my guess" but I think most of them are educated guesses and things we can safely assume but don't know for sure.

◱ **Reply Share Report Save**

> **destroy_all_emmas46** ⊠ 765 points · 7 months ago
> Thank you for your post. I understand there's no real "answers" here but this explains a lot for me, thanks.
> ◱ **Reply Share Report Save**

> **DJPENDEJO** ⊠ 448 points · 7 months ago
> | neither kind of technology actually exists (that we know of) so it's hard to say.
> "That we know of" is the important thing here. Ash's dead man switch video already told us that CO is not just a pharmaceutical company. They're AT LEAST making weapons, probably for the US government. CO needs to

be investigated (which will never happen because, you know, we're a corporatocracy).

⊡ **Reply Share Report Save**

> **themostboringdystopia** ⊠ 158 points • 7 months ago
>
> It's crazy that the claim "CO is making weapons for the US government" is a valid accusation now and not just some backwater youtube conspiracy channel clickbait. This is the darkest timeline.
>
> ⊡ **Reply Share Report Save**

> **slickerpunch** ⊠ 85 points • 7 months ago
>
> Wild that CO is out here like "lets spend millions of dollars to put cameras in peoples eyeballs" when they somehow don't have the money to lower the cost of their drugs. We're simultaneously in the most boring dystopia and the wildest of times.
>
> ⊡ **Reply Share Report Save**

> > **themostboringdystopia** ⊠ 62 points • 7 months ago
> >
> > see my username :)
> >
> > ⊡ **Reply Share Report Save**

> > > **slickerpunch** ⊠ 15 points • 7 months ago
> > >
> > > Haha, nice! Wish that it wasn't an applicable description of the world we live in, but here we are.
> > >
> > > ⊡ **Reply Share Report Save**

> > > > **mimilkshakemio0165** ⊠ 14 points • 7 months ago

|It was the most boring dystopia, it was the wildest of times.

-Charles Dickens

🖅 **Reply Share Report Save**

gingerbreadgnocchi ⊠ 3 points • 7 months ago

Eat Lawson Rich - Albert Einstein

🖅 **Reply Share Report Save**

tahngyjumahnji2 ⊠ 212 points • 7 months ago

Counter-Point: The entire video was faked, and all of those answers are just willful thinking. We already know that Ash has deepfake tech, how hard can it be to stage a kidnapping and map his face onto one of her friends?

What is more likely, that she was some black ops badass and a cabal of the richest men in the world were willing to kidnap and torture her, or she put on a play? Occam's Razor.

🖅 **Reply Share Report Save**

sockandbowloff ⊠ 72 points • 7 months ago

How did I know I'd find a comment like this here? Deepfaking leaves a digital footprint. You might not be able to remove the deepfake mask but you can tell when it is being used. Lawson was not deepfaked in that vid. Sorry to burst your bootlicker bubble.

🖅 **Reply Share Report Save**

radmadladwaradpad ⊠ 48 points • 7 months ago

On any Ash thread, you'll find the same five pro-Ash comments and the same five anti-Ash comments, just repeated over and over with slight variations. It's a circlejerk for sure.

⊡ **Reply Share Report Save**

staygoldbronyboy ⊗ 21 points • 7 months ago
|On any Reddit thread, you'll find the same five comments, just repeated over and over with slight variations. It's a circlejerk for sure.FTFY

⊡ **Reply Share Report Save**

Mangovikingfuneral ⊗ 10 points • 7 months ago
|On the internet, you'll find the same five comments, just repeated over and over with slight variations. It's a circlejerk for sure. FTFYFR

⊡ **Reply Share Report Save**

g-o-r-g-e-a-n-d-f-e-a-s-t ⊗ 52 points • 7 months ago
How you be in EVERY thread talking about "counter point" this and "counter point" that? Get your undergraduate waxing poetic ass TFO

⊡ **Reply Share Report Save**

tahngyjumahnji2 ⊗ 16 points • 7 months ago
Just playing devil's advocate. Everyone in this sub is so up Ash's asshole all the time that someone has to.

⊡ **Reply Share Report Save**

freebaglebitez ⊗ 35 points • 7 months ago
How does this dumbshit comment have so much karma? And it directly contradicts the parent comment. Redditors are dumb af.

⊡ **Reply Share Report Save**

tahngyjumahnji2 ⊗ 22 points · 7 months ago

Reddit is not a hivemind. Some amount of people agree with the parent comment, some amount of people agree with me. It's called society? YOU'RE the one whose "dumb af".

⊡ **Reply Share Report Save**

> **freebaglebitez** ⊗ 17 points · 7 months ago
> |who's
> Maybe get better grammar if you're going to correct me, bumblenuts.
> Not only that, but it's worth mentioning, 5x more people agree with the other poster than you.
> ⊡ **Reply Share Report Save**
>
>> **tahngyjumahnji2** ⊗ 11 points · 7 months ago
>> |You should have better grammar if you're going to correct me
>> And it's not even grammar, it's spelling.
>> ⊡ **Reply Share Report Save**
>>
>>> **redneck_bluestate24** ⊗ 7 points · 7 months ago
>>> BOTH of you are insufferable jfc
>>> ⊡ **Reply Share Report Save**

bombXglossy ⊗ 339 points · 7 months ago

FFS how isn't this guy in jail already

⊡ **Reply Share Report Save**

> **burnallbootlickersVVVVV** ⊗ 183 points · 7 months

The rich play by a different set of rules. Note how the day after Ash's murder supposedly happened, Rich left the country and hasn't been back since. Police can't do much if there's not enough to charge him and it's not like they're going to extradite him just to ask questions. He's Lawson fucking Rich. He doesn't even have to defend himself, just let the shitstorm ride out until people inevitably forget.
⊡ **Reply Share Report Save**

> **nocontextsubtext** ⊠ 99 points • 7 months ago
> rules for thee, not for me
> ⊡ **Reply Share Report Save**

subparcornoncob ⊠ 6 points • 7 months ago
because he didn't do anything wrong
⊡ **Reply Share Report Save**

> **jennifersomebody** ⊠ 66 points • 7 months
> ohhHH BOY get ready for a HOT TAKE guys
> ⊡ **Reply Share Report Save**

> > **subparcornoncob** ⊠ -2 points • 7 months ago
> > if some bitch breaks into my house, i have a right to defend myself
> > ⊡ **Reply Share Report Save**

> > > **jennifersomebody** ⊠ 45 points • 7 months
> > > Does "defending yourself" include kidnapping someone, stripping them naked, implying that you'll torture them until they kill themselves, and then disposing of the body and fleeing the country?
> > > In that case, no, you don't have the right to defend yourself.

⊡ **Reply Share Report Save**

subparcornoncob ⊠ -8 points · 7 months ago
he didn't kill her, case closed
⊡ **Reply Share Report Save**

jennifersomebody ⊠ 41 points · 7 months
Did you hear that detective? Private Dick Corncob over here closed the case! You guys can go home!
⊡ **Reply Share Report Save**

jennifersomebody ⊠ 211 points · 7 months
If you want to do something about it, and you're in the area, people are staging a sit-in starting August 31st at Lawson Rich's estate! He's not currently there, but they plan to occupy his property until he's brought to justice! **Click the link** for details.
⊡ **Reply Share Report Save**

[twitch.tv]

STREAM CHAT

8:43:22 **terminatoretyo:** day 7 of peaceful protest: nothing has been accomplished

8:43:26 **terminatoretyo:** but lets all pat ourselves on the back for doing SOMETHING yeah?

8:43:30 **terminatoretyo:** pathetic

8:43:50 **Marcwithack481:** what do you think they should do then

8:43:58 **Marcwithack481:** not everyone can be ash bro

8:44:10 **terminatoretyo:** burn his fucking house down idk

8:44:16 **terminatoretyo:** SOMETHING

8:44:22 **terminatoretyo:** assholes gotten away with murder and were all just like

8:44:28 **terminatoretyo:** "were sitting on his lawn were doing all we can!"

8:44:43 **Raggerund124:** i mean burning down his house would be helping him get rid of the evidence i think

8:44:49 **Raggerund124:** if its a crime scene

8:44:55 **Raggerund124:** it helps him get rid of any evidence

8:45:30 **inboxfullaphish:** its not a crime scene tho

8:45:38 **inboxfullaphish:** thats part of the problem isnt it

8:45:43 **inboxfullaphish:** police didnt even really investigate

8:45:50 **terminatoretyo:** so everyone storm his house

8:45:57 **terminatoretyo:** and try to find this fucking torture room he has

8:46:03 **terminatoretyo:** wouldnt that corroborate ashs video

8:46:09 **terminatoretyo:** who has a designated TORTURE ROOM in their house?

8:46:19 **Raggerund124:** a hundred people rummaging through his house would taint any evidence i think

8:46:31 **Raggerund124**: idk IANAL

8:46:40 **terminatoretyo**: we know you anal bro

8:46:48 **terminatoretyo**: youre getting fita by lawson rich as we speak

8:46:55 **terminatoretyo**: we all are

8:47:06 **Raggerund124**: I Am Not A Lawyer*

8:47:24 **terminatoretyo**: i know what acronyms are dumbshit im just making a joke

8:47:49 **OligarchOmelette**: if you dont think LR had a TEAM of professionals come by

8:47:57 **OligarchOmelette**: to scrub his house of any evidence

8:48:18 **OligarchOmelette**: then i have some land to sell you

8:49:25 **inboxfullaphish**: look at mr pennybags over here

8:49:32 **inboxfullaphish**: owning LAND? In 2022?

8:49:36 **inboxfullaphish**: maybe we should eat you

8:49:47 **OligarchOmelette**: eat this ass ;)

8:49:55 **inboxfullaphish**: eating ass and taking names

8:49:59 **stacysmomissadom**: how many people are streaming, you think?

8:50:02 **terminatoretyo**: idk, 30? 40?

8:50:10 **terminatoretyo**: twitch home page is filled with streams of the sitin atm

8:50:29 **stacysmomissadom**: do you guys have any other streams open

8:50:35 **stacysmomissadom**: or are you just watching shiv

8:50:42 **unionizeemberi**: i have like eight open

8:50:49 **unionizeemberi**: switching between them

8:50:55 **unionizeemberi**: i learned my lesson when they were looking for david whites body

8:51:12 **stacysmomissadom**: wym

8:51:14 **tallahasseessahallat**: doesnt seem like theres many cops there

8:51:18 **unionizeemberi**: i was only watching yasho's stream

8:51:27 **unionizeemberi**: when all that shit was going down

8:51:33 **unionizeemberi**: and totally missed peeps finding the money

8:51:39 **unionizeemberi**: and getting arrested

8:51:58 **OligarchOmelette**: you didnt miss much

8:52:04 **L9_Savannah**: i was in peeps stream

8:52:09 **L9_Savannah**: vid caught a glimpse of their bodies and then stream went dark

8:52:15 **L9_Savannah**: wasnt much to see

8:52:34 **unionizeemberi**: yeah but yall were a part of that moment

8:52:45 **unionizeemberi**: like truly a part of history

8:52:57 **terminatoretyo**: if youre looking for a repeat

8:53:00 **terminatoretyo**: sorry to tell you dude

8:53:06 **terminatoretyo**: but nothing like thats gonna happen here

8:53:17 **L9_Savannah**: i mean

8:53:19 **L9_Savannah**: were all part of this movement right

8:53:19 **tallahasseessahallat**: its not like he has security there either

8:53:31 **L9_Savannah**: i assume youre not on the specials menu or anything

8:53:38 **unionizeemberi**: speak for yourself :P

8:53:49 **unionizeemberi**: im typing this from my mansion in dubai as we speak

8:53:59 **L9_Savannah**: your un is unionize emberi

8:54:03 **L9_Savannah**: youre one of us

8:54:09 **OligarchOmelette**: ONE OF US

8:54:14 **stacysmomissadom**: ONE OF US

8:54:17 **tallahassee sahabat**: uh guys you watching jshrek's stream?

8:54:21 **Raggerund124**: ONE OF US

8:54:30 **unionizeemberi**: true XD

8:54:32 **tallahasseessahallat**: theyre talking about pushing past the barricade

8:54:36 **unionizeemberi**: betrayed by my own username

8:54:40 **Raggerund124**: what are we chanting about?

8:54:43 **terminatoretyo**: tall, fr?

8:54:50 **joshfrank5610**: yup, jshrek, wahkka and laurenx are making the rounds seeing who's down

8:54:52 **terminatoretyo**: lmao nothings gonna happen jshreks a punk

8:54:58 **Raggerund124**: okay okay this is what im talking about

8:55:02 **Raggerund124**: FTP ACAB ETR

8:55:06 **thatliqlindsay11**: have you guys seen that medium post going around

8:55:09 **thatliqlindsay11**: where that karen is trying to claim that bootlicker is a slur

8:55:15 **terminatoretyo**: yeah dude its been trending for like 3 days

8:55:18 **L9_Savannah**: LMAO NO

8:55:20 **L9_Savannah**: for real?

8:55:25 **terminatoretyo**: who even knows anymore

8:55:27 **L9_Savannah**: link plz

8:55:30 **terminatoretyo**: reality is satire and everything is permitted and nothing is genuine

8:55:32 **terminatoretyo**: and has been for 7 years

8:55:32 **unionizeemberi**: just google it

8:55:35 **unionizeemberi**: click the first result

8:55:35 **tallahasseessahallat**: 8 cops cant keep 100 people from just storming the place

8:55:39 **unionizeemberi**: is this your first time using the internet?

8:55:47 **tallahasseessahallat**: if they really wanted to

8:55:53 **L9_Savannah**: jeez alright i just asked a question

8:56:05 **terminatoretyo**: doesnt matter if its satire

8:56:11 **terminatoretyo**: some if not all of the people who agree with the post

8:56:13 **terminatoretyo**: are def real

8:56:21 **unionizeemberi**: i dont understand

8:56:28 **unionizeemberi**: are people proud of the fact that theyre subservient?

8:56:29 **joshfrank5610**: guys you really should be watching jshreks stream

8:56:33 **unionizeemberi**: are they proud theyre wage slaves?

8:56:37 **joshfrank5610**: theyre about to move

8:56:40 **terminatoretyo**: everyones convinced theyre just "temporarily embarrassed millionaires"

8:56:45 **terminatoretyo**: and that one day theyll be the next lawson rich

8:56:49 **unionizeemberi**: the american dream is a lie

8:56:51 **terminatoretyo**: not realizing that people like rich exert their power

8:56:55 **terminatoretyo**: to make sure people like us never even get out the gutter

8:57:04 **joshfrank5610**: theyre moving

8:57:05 **L9_Savannah**: will i get cancelled for tweeting "ok bootlicker" atb?

8:57:09 **Raggerund124**: THERE WE GO

8:57:11 **joshfrank5610**: THEYRE DOING IT

8:57:14 **tallahasseessahallat**: hell yes this is what i was saying

8:57:16 **terminatoretyo**: guess i was wrong huh

8:57:18 **L9_Savannah**: theyre going to get their asses shot

8:57:22 **OligarchOmelette**: take this motherfucker down

8:57:25 **terminatoretyo**: whats the time frame on police opening fire

8:57:30 **unionizeemberi**: FOR ASH

8:57:37 **joshfrank5610**: jfc

8:57:40 **L9_Savannah**: WHO THE FUCK IS SHOOTING

8:57:42 **Marcwithack481**: wow that was quick

8:57:43 **terminatoretyo**: who had 20 seconds? anyone?

8:57:50 **inboxfullaphish**: what kinda fucking police state do you guys live in

8:57:57 **terminatoretyo**: streams down

8:58:00 **Marcwithack481**: stream down for anyone else?

8:58:03 **joshfrank5610**: ALL the streams are down

8:58:07 **OligarchOmelette**: theyre gonna kill em all

8:58:12 **joshfrank5610**: literally all 8 streams i had open are down

8:58:07 **OligarchOmelette**: how would they even do that?

8:58:45 **OligarchOmelette**: anyone?

8:59:23 **OligarchOmelette**: hello?

9:05:13 **terminatoretyo**: never seen twitch chat go down like that before

9:05:20 **joshfrank5610**: streams seem to be back back up as well

9:05:21 **Marcwithack481**: wht the hell was that?

9:05:24 **L9_Savannah**: are they fucking LOOTING richs house?

9:05:31 **terminatoretyo**: why wouldnt they be

9:05:35 **Raggerund124**: wasnt this supposed to be about finding evidence rich killed ash

9:05:42 **unionizeemberi**: i mean it wasnt really about anything

9:05:49 **unionizeemberi**: it wasnt planned it was just supposed to be a sitin

9:05:54 **joshfrank5610**: laurenx is saying three people were shot

9:05:56 **unionizeemberi**: jfc

9:05:59 **joshfrank5610**: and the cops were swarmed by some protestors

9:06:08 **joshfrank5610**: while others ran into the house

9:06:12 **terminatoretyo**: i mean . . . his house looks like it did in ashs video

9:06:15 **L9_Savannah**: theyre really going at it

9:06:19 **terminatoretyo**: is that proof enough that the vid was real?

9:06:26 **Marcwithack481**: i mean it depends?

9:06:27 **L9_Savannah**: youre going to the FRIDGE? WHY?????

9:06:29 **L9_Savannah**: GO TO THE BEDROOM YA IDJITS

9:06:32 **Marcwithack481:** if no one knows what the inside of his house looks like, yeah

9:06:38 **unionizeemberi:** OH THE THING

9:06:41 **Marcwithack481:** if rich has done an episode of cribs or something and its already on video, then no

9:06:44 **unionizeemberi:** THE THING SHE SHOT BEHIND THE FRIDGE

9:06:48 **terminatoretyo:** whats cribs?

9:06:50 **Raggerund124:** OH SHII

9:06:54 **Marcwithack481:** jesus im old

9:06:56 **L9_Savannah:** THE THING

9:06:57 **Marcwithack481:** nvm

9:06:59 **tallahasseessahallat:** go find the torture room

9:07:05 **L9_Savannah:** what the hell is it

9:07:08 **tallahasseessahallat:** that would be the most convincing thing dont you think

9:07:11 **terminatoretyo:** theyre really destroying the place

9:07:14 **terminatoretyo:** good for them

9:07:16 **Raggerund124:** what just happened

9:07:19 **Marcwithack481:** streams down again

9:07:22 **Raggerund124:** did you guys see that

9:07:25 **Raggerund124:** right before the feed cut out

9:07:28 **Marcwithack481:** what is the lge shitty by his place or what

9:07:33 **L9_Savannah:** streams down

9:07:36 **joshfrank5610:** the house exploded

9:07:41 **unionizeemberi:** what??????

9:07:43 **OligarchOmelette:** what

9:07:48 **joshfrank5610:** jfcOPEN ANOTHER STREAM

9:07:52 **L9_Savannah:** what do you mean the house exploded

9:07:59 **joshfrank5610:** THE HOUSE FUCKING EXPLODED

[imgur.com]

An album comparing Lawson Rich's house in Ash's video VS. the protester's videos

wespeakspanglishhere
6,216 views · 6h

⊠
⊠
⊠
⊠
⊠
⊠
⊠
⊠
⊠
⊠

[Load 72 more images]

Sign in to leave a comment   Sign in
[Sign up]

25 COMMENTS

───────────────────────────────

isaiphuckett · 1h via **Android**
What's the significance of this?
▲ **178** ▼ | — Collapse Replies

    biilllliiliiliill · 1h

Before Ash's video, no footage existed of the inside of
Lawson Rich's house. The
twitch streams prove that Ash's video was not faked.
Lawson Rich kidnapped and
killed a woman and this album corroborates that.
▲ 99 ▼ | + 1 reply

pizzaemojiiballs · 1h via **Android**
⊠
▲ 83 ▼ | + 2 replies

eatmemesshartjeans · 1h via **iPhone**
it proves people know how to use photoshop
▲ 41 ▼ | + 4 replies

gon0horribletea · 1h via **iPhone**
⊠
▲ 155 ▼ | + 5 replies

donglelikebeckham · 1h via **Android**
⊠
▲ 142 ▼ | + 2 replies

lossofbosssauce · 33m
17-23 seals the deal for me. Digital photo frame, photos cycle in
the same order. Ash's dead man's switch video was real.
▲ 139 ▼ | — Collapse Replies

thefineartoffarting · 19m via Android
⊠
▲ 85 ▼ | + 3 replies

georgewhorewell1948 · 16m via Android
⊠

▲ 65 ▼ | + 2 replies

lilyanndarkham491 · 15m
not only that, but reverse img search shows that none of
those photos of Rich and his
fam are online at all. It would be impossible to fake.
▲ 65 ▼ | + 1 reply

artisinalbongwater · 1h via **iPhone**
fake news
▲ 125 ▼ | — Collapse Replies

    rumandcokeham666 · 1h via **iPhone**
    ⊠
    ▲ 54 ▼ | + 1 reply

    createauser9342017 · 1h via **Android**
    ⊠
    ▲ 32 ▼ |

    sitandspin90005 · 50m via **Android**
    ⊠
    ▲ 29 ▼ |

    pisscityshartville · 45m via **Android**
    ⊠
    ▲ 11 ▼ |

[twitter.com]

Trending · **Lawson Rich** · 300.1K tweets

CNN @CNN · **September 7**

Explosion at Lawson Rich's Connecticut home leaves
31 dead, 64 injured (cnn.com)

---

112 Replies   **55 Retweets**   **762 Likes**

Chad Preston @badhocwifi2077 · **September 7**

Lawson Rich's body count increases by the day. Make
no mistake, he blew up his house to DESTROY THE
EVIDENCE. This was not an attack against Rich, this
was an attack BY Rich. 30 people died. When will he
be held accountable?

---

6 Replies   **4 Retweets**   **5 Likes**

The WashingtonPost @washingtonpost · **September 7**

Emberi stock prices plummet as customers boycotting
the company call for an investigation of CEO Lawson
Rich (washingtonpost.com)

---

99 Replies   **147 Retweets**   **198 Likes**

Karl Barx @w00fw00fcomrade · September 7
Replying to @w00fw00fcomrade

Over the years our benefits have been stripped and
our pay has stagnated as Lawson Rich has made
HUNDREDS of billions of dollars . . . in the face of his
flagrant disregard for life and the law, that stops now.
Please support us by NOT crossing the picket line!
(2/2)

1 Reply   **11 Retweets**   **15 Likes**

Karl Barx @w00fw00fcomrade · September 7

I've worked at the Hillside Feed Yourself location for
four years. Me and my coworkers are planning on
striking, starting tomorrow morning, until we are
provided with a living wage AND Lawson Rich steps
down as Emberi CEO . . . (1/2)

3 Replies   **19 Retweets**   **20 Likes**

Josh Roosevelt @defnotarushnbot20XX · September 7

Let's call the raid on Lawson Rich's estate what it is . . .
a TERRORIST ATTACK!!! These communists want
to destroy our way of life and hate the idea of AMERICA

ITSELF!!! WONT OUR GOVT DO SOMETHING!!!

---

1 Reply   **Retweet**   **1 Like**

NEWSBYCO @NEWSBYCONEWS · September 7

Emberi employees nationwide plan to strike September
8th, sparked by murder allegations against Emberi
CEO Lawson Rich and claims of stagnating benefits
and pay (newsbyconews.com)

---

39 Replies   **29 Retweets**   **187 Likes**

Bootstrap Security @Bootstrapsecurity · September 7

Protect yourself and your assets with bootstrap security!
Sign up for our PREMIUM PLATINUM Security
Package today!

Promoted by Bootstrap Security

Haisley Writes Words @hirehaisleystb · September 7

Why hasn't Lawson Rich been arrested? Why hasn't he
shown his face after being accused of murder and after
his house freaking EXPLODED? It's almost like . . .
laws exist for the poor and disenfranchised, but
not for the rich? No . . . that couldn't be it.

---

8 Replies **3 Retweets** **22 Likes**

Breitbart News @BreitbartNews · September 7

True American Patriot Lawson Rich, employer of more
than a million Americans, under fire by deep state
operatives after senseless terrorist attack leaves him
homeless (breitbart.com)

---

59 Replies **72 Retweets** **199 Likes**

Sienna Black @tortugablack227 · September 7
Replying to @tortugablack227

Emberi is ALREADY hurting, and we've BARELY
started. Let's remind them that WE, THE WORKERS,
have the power and that they owe all of their success
to US. NOT Lawson Rich. DO NOT BREAK THE
PICKET LINE, SUPPORT LOCAL BUSINESSES
INSTEAD! (2/2)

---

5 Replies **6 Retweets** **19 Likes**

Sienna Black @tortugablack227 · September 7

This only works if we boycott ALL Emberi owned
companies. WE / FY / SU — NO GO! DO NOT GIVE

ANY OF THESE COMPANIES ANY MONEY UNTIL
THEY HOLD LAWSON RICH ACCOUNTABLE AND
GIVE THE WORKERS THAT BUILT EMBERI WHAT
THEY'RE OWED! (1/2)

---

8 Replies   **10 Retweets**   **25 Likes**

[mNeuron app screenshot]

price
Online

the board is weighing its options
8:00 AM

> such as
> 8:00 AM

holding a vote of no confidence
8:00 AM

and instilling me as ceo
8:00 AM

> not enough
> 8:00 AM

thats what they want
8:01 AM

they want rich gone
8:01 AM

and were considering whether that will work for us
8:01 AM

> they also want $20/hr, unions, and healthcare
> 8:01 AM

absolutely not

8:01 AM

consider it
8:01 AM

the writing is on the wall
8:01 AM

and it may be time to make concessions
8:02 AM

if we want to weather this
8:02 AM

is CO going to do the same?
8:05 AM

well CO employees are salaried
8:05 AM

and already have healthcare
8:05 AM

why
8:05 AM

CO isn't like FY
8:06 AM

we need the best and brightest
8:06 AM

not just someone who can work a register
8:06 AM

SU employees aren't salaried
8:06 AM

and they're capped at 29/hr weeks
8:07 AM

so no healthcare
8:07 AM

listen i dont want to make this a pissing contest
8:07 AM

but that's why CO consistently outperforms SU
8:07 AM

and why your retention is terrible
8:07 AM

whats your point
8:07 AM

we're giving everyone a 15% pay raise
8:08 AM

and letting them unionize
8:08 AM

fuck off
8:12 AM

are you trying to fuck us with this
8:12 AM

no thats what im saying
8:13 AM

this isn't about optics
8:13 AM

well it is but not in the way youre thinking
8:13 AM

is this because rich said you didnt have balls
8:15 AM

because you already blew up his fucking house
8:15 AM

that's part of it
8:16 AM

fuck you
8:18 AM

this isn't about that
8:19 AM

this is because i'm still on the specials menu
8:19 AM

as are you
8:19 AM

as is the entire board of emberi
8:20 AM

don't remind me

8:25 AM

bootstraps bleeding me fucking dry
8:25 AM

and im not even that high a target
8:26 AM

your bounty is 5 mil
8:27 AM

bounty for the entire board is 35 mil
8:27 AM

id think again
8:27 AM

thats not that much
8:28 AM

people are taking contracts for less
8:29 AM

something like 30% of people on the sm have been taken out
8:30 AM

jeeeesus
8:33 AM

fucking animals
8:33 AM

why are you bringing this up
8:34 AM

covington was on the sm when it came out
8:35 AM

and now he's not
8:35 AM

fuck that
8:37 AM

and fuck you
8:37 AM

im not donating all my money to those mongrels
8:38 AM

YOU DONT HAVE TO
8:38 AM

but be realistic
8:38 AM

holding a "vote of no confidence"
8:38 AM

isnt going to do jack shit to stop this and you know it
8:38 AM

they want rich gone
8:40 AM

well get rid of him
8:40 AM

theyll end their strike
8:40 AM

its called compromise
8:40 AM

did you see what happened to betsy?
8:41 AM

did you see what happened to rocco
8:41 AM

ash ate his damn balls
8:41 AM

we're way past compromising with these people
8:41 AM

what does this have to do with you
8:44 AM

why are we talking right now
8:44 AM

i have a proposal
8:45 AM

thatll benefit both of us
8:45 AM

keep talking
8:46 AM

the first part of which
8:46 AM

is im going to make a move on rich
8:46 AM

and i wanted to make sure im not stepping on any toes
8:46 AM

fuck rich
8:50 AM

were way past that
8:50 AM

what do you have in mind
8:50 AM

the registry
8:51 AM

it doesnt work the way we want it to
8:51 AM

but for finding lawson rich . . .
8:51 AM

itll work fine
8:52 AM

bullshit
8:52 AM

it works?
8:52 AM

like i said
8:52 AM

not for what we made it for
8:53 AM

but it can find one person easily enough
8:53 AM

and then?
8:54 AM

and as soon as you give the okay
8:55 AM

i can launch the website thats already made
8:55 AM

that will tell the entire world where lawson rich is
8:55 AM

down to the square foot
8:55 AM

updated, in real time, in perpetuity
8:55 AM

and let the animals take care of him
8:57 AM

yes
8:57 AM

and keep our hands clean of the whole thing

8:57 AM

and it wont be traced back to us?
8:59 AM

no chance
9:00 AM

and theoretically
9:01 AM

you wouldnt even need to tell the board about this
9:01 AM

if you can guarantee my safety
9:01 AM

if it cant be traced back to you
9:03 AM

then why are you worried about that?
9:03 AM

dont be coy
9:04 AM

emberi knows about richs house
9:04 AM

even if no one else does
9:04 AM

you know more than you let on
9:04 AM

dont worry about emberi
9:05 AM

with rich gone, i AM emberi
9:05 AM

alright then
9:06 AM

as soon as rich is taken out
9:06 AM

we also have an astroturf campaign set up
9:06 AM

smart
9:07 AM

websites live
9:10 AM

huh
9:10 AM

hong kong
9:11 AM

hes been everywhere over the past week
9:11 AM

who knows where hell be tomorrow
9:11 AM

you said that was the first step
9:12 AM

                              youre not going to like the next one
                                                      9:13 AM

what
9:14 AM

                                    give them what they want
                                                  9:14 AM

even if i agreed
9:15 AM

id never be able to convince the board
9:15 AM

                                    this isnt about compromise
                                                  9:16 AM

                                    this is about concessions
                                                  9:16 AM

                                    in the interest of survival
                                                  9:16 AM

                    how long can emberi survive a company-wide strike
                                                              9:16 AM

                                          and mass boycotts
                                                  9:16 AM

were hurting
9:17 AM

badly
9:17 AM

exactly
9:18 AM

and what happens if you oust rich
9:18 AM

and the strikes dont stop
9:18 AM

we look weak
9:19 AM

see, you get it
9:20 AM

but if we get emberi and CO
9:20 AM

and some of the other bigger corps on board
9:21 AM

we convince them theyve won
9:22 AM

we get our names off the sm
9:22 AM

we kneecap the movement
9:22 AM

and we get back to normal
9:23 AM

ill never be able to convince the board
9:26 AM

i thought you said you WERE emberi
9:26 AM

some things still need to go through the board
9:27 AM

what if we split the $$$ in richs offshore accounts
9:28 AM

interesting
9:29 AM

howd you get access?
9:30 AM

a magician never reveals their secrets
9:31 AM

but the second the animals take care of rich
9:31 AM

that money can be disbursed among the emberi board, myself, and a
few others
9:32 AM

how much?
9:35 AM

160, easy

9:35 AM

10 each
9:36 AM

its not nothing
9:37 AM

but is it enough?
9:37 AM

this isnt stock or taxable income
9:38 AM

its 10b liquid, untraceable cash
9:38 AM

dont pretend like that isnt 10x your net worth
9:39 AM

i dont know if itll be enough
9:45 AM

to convince them
9:45 AM

one more thing
9:46 AM

rich had a 5% stake in NEON
9:46 AM

which you can distribute as you see fit
9:46 AM

NEON?
9:55 AM

isnt that theoretical?
9:55 AM

were in the testing phases now
9:55 AM

should be ready within the next 4-5 years
9:56 AM

ill talk to the board
9:57 AM

this is a more than generous offer
9:57 AM

dont be stupid
9:57 AM

i think you might be overreacting
9:59 AM

we might not need to take such drastic measures
10:00 AM

said the king with his neck in the guillotine
10:01 AM

youre fucking yourself here
10:01 AM

im trying to help
10:01 AM

dont overstep, guy
10:02 AM

you know what
10:02 AM

ive placated you long enough
10:03 AM

emberi is MY company and you will not tell me how to
run it
10:03 AM

there will be no deal
10:03 AM

and you can fuck off to your town house
10:03 AM

before i call the tabloids to tell them what you did
10:04 AM

you fucked up
10:04 AM

i tried the carrot
10:04 AM

because it would have worked out better for both of us
10:04 AM

but heres the stick

10:04 AM

i know about cannes
10:05 AM

i know about the factories in pennsylvania
10:05 AM

i know about the stash house in dublin
10:05 AM

and the penthouse in dubai
10:05 AM

i know what you did to silence all those women
10:05 AM

who were about to come forward against rich
10:05 AM

in 2015
10:06 AM

I know about ACAI
10:06 AM

i know all your fucking dirty little secrets
10:06 AM

i even know what happened to emma
10:06 AM

i have ALL the receipts
10:06 AM

so dont fucking test me
10:06 AM

well talk tomorrow
10:06 AM

dont do anything rash
10:06 AM

thats what i fucking thought
10:10 AM

[twitter.com]

← Trends

Trending in United States
#RIPRICH
235.4K Tweets

Trending in United States
$20/hr
Trending with: Emberi

Trending in United States
Emberi
Trending with: Unionized

Trending in United States
Citizen One
Trending with: Unionized

Trending in United States
#SundayFunday
5,922 Tweets

Trending in United States
#EndTheStrikes
70.8K Tweets

Trending in United States
#WhatHappenedToEmma
16.8K Tweets

Trending in United States
Hong Kong
Trending with: Lawson Rich

Trending in United States
#mNeuronLeaks
60.9K Tweets

Trending in United States
#BackToWork
70.7K Tweets

Trending in United States
#WhoIsEmma
14.4K Tweets

Trending in United States
Rip Price
Trending with: Suicide

Trending in United States
#OpenEmberiNow
70.8K Tweets

Trending in United States
#WeAteTheRich
71.1K Tweets

Trending in United States
#RIPPRICEDIDNTKILLHIMSELF
12.5K Tweets

Trending in United States
#THANKYOUASH
15.5K Tweets

Trending in United States

#BuyBackEmberiStock
70.9K Tweets

Trending in United States
Guy Capps
Trending with: killed Rip Price, right?

Trending in United States
#SundaeFundae
4,774 Tweets

Somebody's Last Words

This is not the end of the story.

In the inevitable movie that gets made about Ash Whatever, this is where the credits will roll. But this is not the end of the story. You might think that one would have already been made, or at least put into pre-production, but they don't know how to frame Ash's story. They don't know who to make the villain, or the protagonist, or the anti-hero. Ash's story is a complicated one. All you know is that this is not the end.

In any case, in the inevitable movie or limited series that gets made, this is where faces in frozen frame will flash on the screen. This is where walls of text will tell you what happened after the conversation between Rip Price and Guy Capps. As if you don't remember.

Or maybe it will be a podcast. Probably there will be a podcast. Probably there are already podcasts. This is where the narrator with the pleasing voice tells you that on September 27th, 2022, the website "wtfislawsonrichrn.com" went live. It told the world that Lawson Rich was in a secluded mansion on Victoria Peak, home to Hong Kong's most extravagant and overpriced homes. Hours later, he was dead. His death was not livestreamed. It is unknown who killed Lawson Rich or how many or how, but hours later his body was found hanging from the roof of the Peak Tower, a shopping complex and tourist attraction nearby. Despite the presence of many security cameras, no footage exists of the individuals who killed Lawson Rich.

Chinese authorities confirmed the body to be Lawson Rich. Whether or not you trust the Chinese authorities is up to you.

The next day, a spokesperson for Emberi addressed the company and its shareholders through a livestream. The spokesperson announced that Emberi would acquiesce to its employees and grant them all a base pay of twenty dollars an hour, increased PTO, healthcare across the board, and would no longer take actions to prevent them from unionizing.

During the strikes Emberi's stock price dropped from $3,512/share to $821/share. At the news of Lawson Rich's death, Emberi stock rose to 70 percent of where it had been before Ash's death, or $2,550 . After the announcements that employee benefits would be increased, the stock dipped back down by 40 percent, to $1,525 . But since then, it has steadily risen to where it is nearly the price it was before Lawson Rich killed Ash Whatever—$3,391/share. As of December, 2022, Emberi has gone back to posting record profits every month as confidence in the company has been restored.

On September 28th, 2022, NEWSBYCO broke the news that Rip Price had committed suicide. He was found in his Medina, Washington, home by his wife. In the days that followed, it was reported that he hung himself from the rafters in his bedroom and shot himself twice in the head.

You find that suspicious. You do not think that Rip Price killed himself. But after the hashtags died and the news cycle cycled the average person forgot Rip Price's name and no investigations were opened. Eventually, you also forget about Rip Price.

After Rich's death and the announcement from Emberi management, the astroturfing campaign started and, within days, the strikes ended. Emberi employees went back to work with their increased pay and newfound benefits. People tweeted #wewon and #ashwouldbeproud and #weatetherich like they weren't just thrown crumbs when Ash wanted the whole cake. It was a victory, don't get me wrong. But it was a small victory in a battle that should have raged on, that should be ongoing. But people forgot. People are good at forgetting.

On October 3rd, 2022, screenshots of Guy Capp's and Rip Price's mNeuron logs were released online, maybe by a whistleblower, maybe by a hacker, maybe by Capps himself. The veracity of the logs was argued until people forgot about that too. mNeuron's stock dropped by 80 percent, to $30/share, at the news that mNeuron was not as secure as its founders stated. But their *stock rebounded as well, and now trades at $212/share. The implication that Guy Capps had a hand in doxxing Rich, that he had a hand in Rich's death, that he killed Rip Price and staged his suicide, all these things came to light and trended and then were forgotten as the world moved on. You forget about them. You try not to, but there's too much going on and the world moves too fast and more and more outrageous and egregious things are happening all around you and there's too much to be angry about and before you know it, you don't think about Guy Capps or Rip Price. You've forgotten what you've forgotten.*

On October 20th, 2022, the pages on the dark web listing the specials menu were scrubbed. People stopped getting paid for the contracts and soon after, people started getting arrested for contracts that had been completed. Normal, everyday people that thought they could get away with what Ash got away with. They couldn't and they didn't. Before it went down, almost half of the specials menu had been taken out.

Guy Capps was never taken out. He is now the CEO of Citizen One.

Someday this will all get made into a movie. A limited series. A podcast. It will be memed out of existence. But what I fear is that people will focus on Ash, on White and Mann and Cadejo and Ragham, on Price and Rich and Guy. They will forget the movement that Ash started, they will forget the discussions she fostered, they will forget that the internet was as integral to Eating the Rich as Ash. The comments, the hashtags, the posts and chat logs. All of it.

The internet is a reflection of us at our worst and best. It is fucked up and beautiful. It is filled with hateful trolls and people with good intentions. It is the worst thing that's happened to us and the best. It is undefinable and scary and irreversibly woven into what society is and shall be. It is the context for Ash's movement, and I have done my best to showcase the good and bad, the repetitive and truly batshit.

Life goes on and on and on. People didn't forget Ash's name—they didn't forget what she did—but they forgot how they felt when they knew they had someone in their corner. They forgot the anger they felt, the righteous anger, at all the powerful assholes fucking them over on a daily basis. They forgot the rush of clicking the link to a new video and seeing someone who had never been held accountable finally getting what they deserved. They forgot what it was like to eat the rich and to see the rich get eaten. They forgot their hunger.

They forgot that this is not a war with an end. This is not something that resolves itself and is ever fixed. It's easy to forget because fighting is hard. It's exhausting. This is a constant struggle, a fight without a knockout, and we need to keep fighting, even if it is in small ways that don't make as big a splash as Ash.

I'm nobody. I'm Somebody but I'm also nobody. You have no reason to listen to me, but I implore you to keep fighting. Donate to the causes you think make a difference. Vote in every election. Not just the presidential, not just in the big ones, but every one. Canvass, converse, convince. But be kind to each other. Support local politicians. Support local businesses. Try to hold the powerful accountable. Speak out loudly and often about injustices you witness. Try your hardest. Hold on to your hunger. Support each other. I won't make a difference. But you can. The collective you, not just the individual.

Don't forget. Stay hungry.

Made in United States
North Haven, CT
26 November 2021

11564010R10178